THE STONE EAGLE

Episode I

P.K. LASKY

Middle Roads Publishing

CONTENTS

MY BROTHER HATED Rome and its legions, the military school, the garrison walls.

Karig called himself a prisoner, a hostage, drug his feet in exercises, refused to speak in Latin or Greek and stood his ground when the master trainer withheld food but not the whip.

The gruff priest tried to purge the demons from my brother's pagan heart.

Karig laughed, ripped the rough-cut metal cross from the priest's unshaved neck and carved the sign of Tiews—god of the Goth warrior—into his own right upper arm.

What began as an arrow pointing north quickly caused Karig's arm to swell and ooze puss. Then came the fever and three days of meaningless babble.

The priest sat by my brother's bedside whispering prayers. The old Greek doctor ladled herbed broth down Karig's throat. Whether the broth or the prayers saved my brother, I would never know.

The infection bent Karig's scar, twisted it so the arrow no longer pointed up but slanted backward along the curve of his developing muscle. It was a scarlet, gnarled mark, something deep and ugly.

Karig did not hide it. Tiews had bent it, he said. The guards could take his rune, but they could not take this.

After death threatened him, Karig hated stronger and harder than before. I only saw the hate, not my brother, and kept my distance. True, we were prisoners of a kind, but for me, our prison was a sanctuary and a window into a bigger world. I found strength in the garrison walls, freedom in the structure, wisdom in the training. Things made sense, at least behind the stacked stones. I saw my future in the legions, wanted to achieve the rank of centurion, and poured my heart into proving myself worthy.

Karig called me a traitor, a coward.

We didn't speak after that.

When I was told of my brother's death, I told myself I didn't care. I blamed him…and his hate.

I was wrong.

In the end, it wasn't Karig's hate that beat him. It was a single moment of hope, a naive trust, and a cold, unforgiving river.

MASTER TRAINER CASSIAN rouses us before the sun, his ox-like mass shaking the floorboards of Junior Barracks C. No need to call us to attention. No need to speak. Master Trainer Cassian strides once down the bunk line and every last cadet is on his feet, spine ramrod straight.

I'm first dressed, first outside, the right and duty of a lead cadet. I count heads as the others line up—only six.

Marius, the youngest of us, rattles around inside, and I have to go back in for him. He's kicked one of his boots under a bunk and can't reach it. I hook it with my training stick, throw the boot out the barrack's door and tell Marius to fetch it on his way to the line.

Slow to start, we march double-time to the open space in front of the trainers' quarters, but we're too late. Junior Barracks A is already in formation, first to muster.

I take my place on my mark. My cadets fall in line behind me.

Thomas faces forward next to me with his chin raised

and a smug look on his hawk-like face. He was first yester-day, too. We've kept a running score. Now he's a point ahead, and Marius will answer for it at the morning meal.

I use my irritation to flush the last bit of sleep from my limbs, then press it down.

Tomorrow's another day.

It's darker than usual, the air crisp. I breathe in, hoping for a hint of fresh-baked bread while we wait. When the breeze is right, the scent wafts from the bakery ovens on the other side of the garrison. Not this morning. Either it's too early, or the bakery has worked through its supplies again. Instead, the slight breeze carries smells from the stables and the refuse collected in grain sacks behind the officer's quarters.

I'm unsure of the hour. There might be a tinge of red above the eastern garrison wall. Either way, sunrise isn't close. A clear sky and three-quarter moon means we could begin drills in the dark, but the trainers steal our night vision by lighting torches that hang from the barracks and surrounding wooden posts. The muster area flickers. It's hard to see past the glare.

Youngsters file in to the right of us. Seniors to our left. Three assistant trainers oversee the process, barking at the youngsters who are last to settle in.

Master Trainer Cassian peers through the dim light at our lines. His round face and bald head glow orange. In daylight, the big man can appear almost jolly, despite standing a head and shoulders taller than any other soldier in the garrison. Without the sun, he's a demon from our first bedtime stories. Not that he needs this to keep our attention. We wait in silence for him to begin.

"The day will bring pain," the master trainer says, his voice tunnel-deep, raspy from a lifetime of shouting orders.

This announcement breaks from the daily pattern, but no one doubts his word.

"You will work until one of you drops to the dirt. Drops and can't pick your sorry, undisciplined backside up off the ground. Earns yourself a ticket to see the Greek."

I sense Thomas straighten. I've heckled him for the last week, telling him to prepare himself. The trainers would try to surprise him, test him early.

I know I'm right. This is it.

The master trainer sweeps an eye over our muster lines then issues commands, "Youngsters, to the stables. Seniors, report to the wall. Move."

Youngsters and seniors hustle to their assigned rotation, the assistant trainers grunting orders as they go. Junior cadets remain in formation in front of the master trainer.

In the commotion, I risk a quick glance at Thomas.

Today, I mouth.

Thomas ignores me.

"Juniors, you're with me," the master trainer says when the others are gone. "Prepare to sweat."

ONCE WE START, there's no stopping—weapons drills, formation drills, marching and standing. By full light, my throat is raw from relaying orders in the early spring cold.

Between evolutions, we march in two-by-two formation around the oval arena, the master trainer supervising from a wooden platform at one end.

"Junior Leader Matthias," Master Trainer Cassian belts across the three hundred feet of open dirt between us, "get your cadets in order."

"Yes, sir." A lead weight drops in my stomach at the rebuke. It's been two drills and eighteen laps since we last broke for water. I've tried to keep a steady pace, but my cadets are tired.

An explanation, not an excuse.

One flick of my training stick across the back of Tradian's calf and the others tighten the file. The stick leaves a mark. It has to, or it's useless.

"Water," the master trainer calls.

We're allowed a short break, the first chance I've had to speak to Thomas. "You ready for this?" I say at the circular fountain.

"Not 'til tomorrow," he says.

Decimus, head cadet of Junior Barracks B, takes his turn at the spout. "I'm with Matthias. Promotion day. Gotta be."

I slap Thomas in the chest. "Told you."

"Not 'til tomorrow."

Thomas talks like he's sure, but he's chewing his lip. He doesn't believe it.

"Back to work," the master trainer orders.

When the sun tilts to the west, the assistant trainers escort the youngsters and seniors into the arena. Whatever they've been up to, as a group they look worn down. Maybe they've been worked as hard as the juniors, but I doubt it.

We partner up for one-on-one wrestling. Older cadets pair with younger ones. Lead cadets fall in with the rest. We're released from our leadership duties.

My stomach gnaws at me. We've trained through the

break-of-fast, through the noon meal. We haven't eaten since the night before. Who knows when food will come, but a cadet is stupid if he lets his stomach distract him.

Eyes forward, I tell myself. *Eat from the plate in front of you.*

My partner—fourth of the rotation—is a bug-eyed boy with an oversized head, eight years old, who pukes on my new calf leather boots a few rounds into our pairing. The kid's stomach is empty. Not much comes out, but the smell packs a punch.

The youngster should quit, except this kid has fight.

Good for him.

He grips me around the waist and shoves his colossal head into my gut, bending me forward, closer to the stench. Acid hits the back of my throat, and I swallow the lump down.

The boy retches again.

I'm the mentor in this pairing—six years older, a lifetime inside the academy—and I'm supposed to be teaching him, pushing without breaking him. But if I don't get out of the huddle, away from the stink, I'll be puking up nothing, too.

Sorry kid.

It's against the rules, but I prepare to sweep his leg from under him. Take him down. End the round early. Thankfully, it doesn't come to that.

The master trainer signals a halt and nods to Assistant Trainer Levius, solemn and sinewed, to inspect the situation. Lev flicks me with his training stick as he passes. He'd seen what I was about to do. Of course, he did. The trainers see everything.

Lev raises the youngster's chin to look into his eyes, then orders the boy to the infirmary. The youngster hangs his head and steps out of the drill line, the first of the day to earn a ticket. The old Greek doctor, Paulopus, will see to the care of the boy's body, but nothing can heal the shame of it. When he shows his face again, the kid will have to fight that much harder, both in the barracks and the arena, to earn back respect.

I hold my body at attention as my eyes follow my fallen opponent. It seems unfair to send a cadet to meet the Greek before he quits on his own. A cadet should be allowed to decide his own fate. But fair is an idea for the weak.

Lev sends a second youngster to go with the first. No cadet walks alone within the garrison. The shamed boy is retching violently now but refuses the arm offered to him. He makes his own way out of the arena's west gate.

"Youngsters dismissed," Master Trainer Cassian says.

Lev orders Drusus, our youngest trainer, to escort the youngsters to the baths, then to the priest for their studies.

It's seventh hour, one horn past noon. The juniors and seniors remain.

The hurt is just beginning.

SWEAT TRICKLES from my shaved head into my eyes. I ignore the sting of it, raise my shield to compensate for my blurred vision, and smile at Thomas across from me. He's my friend, but not in the drill line. I step in to strike.

We are the two oldest junior cadets. Like me, Thomas has earned the top junior rank and holds the honor of lead cadet for his barracks. The trainers pair us often, but that doesn't make us equal.

Thomas is the son of the Camp Prefect. His father is the second highest ranking officer in the garrison. Thomas is a head taller than me, more muscular, a few months older. He has a long reach and a strike like a hammer, a strike that makes an opponent, even a senior, plant his feet and focus.

It must be nice.

I have nothing like that. No special weapon I can rely on in a fight, nothing the other cadets fear. I lack reach and weight and am average in height, so I can't depend on brute strength to crush an opponent. My reflexes and speed make me tough to pin down, but others are faster or have better aim. I work hard. In most areas, I manage, but training doesn't come easily to me. It's no surprise I don't often win on foot. Or on horseback, come to think of it. Or with a spear. At least not outright. Usually it's a draw because I'm too pig-headed to give up.

Thomas will be fifteen tomorrow, the age of promotion into the seniors. He's convinced the trainers will wait until his birthday—it's all about the rules with Thomas—but I don't think so. The master trainer has been watching, assessing. Lev's been hovering. The test is coming.

"Bet they give you the bunk under Nonius," I say between gulps on our next water break. I take my time, make Thomas wait. "You'll have to sleep with your blanket over your nose and mouth."

"Shut up, pebble head. Not 'til tomorrow." Thomas pushes me aside, splashes water over his face and shoves his mouth and beak nose under a spout.

"Drink up. You're gonna need it."

"To your lines," Lev calls.

We race back to the drill lines and wait for instructions.

"*Pungit.*" Jab and defend. "Begin."

For a cadet to promote from the junior to the senior ranks within the academy, he must prove he is ready. He's given a test, a series of trials designed to target his individual weaknesses. No matter what form this gauntlet takes, a show of skill is the first step, the easiest step. A cadet must demonstrate he is physically able and has mastered all the basic training.

The real challenge comes later. The trainers call it a gift, a lesson, hard and always painful. The trainers push the cadet past a breaking point, show him exactly how much he can take, so a boy knows himself, knows what he's capable of.

"Halt," Lev calls.

"A savage pounds his chest and lies to himself before a fight," the master trainer says, while the cadets catch their breath. "A soldier of Rome knows what tools he has."

I hear my father in my ear. He is not a legionnaire, not a citizen, yet his message was the same. "A man can't know his limits if he's never met them." It's not a thing most barbarians tell their sons, but my father is Sakarig the Silent, leader of the Goth auxiliary unit of the region. He is not like most barbarians.

Not everyone passes promotion the first time. Some have to wait a season, have to try again.

"*Super Caput.*" Overhead strikes. "Begin."

Thomas swings his spatha halfheartedly, a beat too slow. He's lagging. Probably thinking about his stomach or the cramp in his left leg. He's favored it for the last two rounds of open sparring.

Any other day, I'd punish the leg until it gave out. It's bad practice to waste an advantage. Not today. Whatever is to come, Thomas will need his limbs for later. I shift and dodge and force Thomas to keep his feet moving. If Thomas stops, his feet will turn to lead.

"You stink like the back end of a goat." Thomas drops his spatha and backs away. "How about cleaning your boot next water break."

"You like that?" I inhale deep. "I've rinsed it twice. Didn't help. I'm used to it now. Puts hair on your chest."

"Try again."

"Cut the chatter," Lev orders.

The sun leans west. The buccina blasts his horn from the south wall of the garrison. It's eighth hour. A body drops along the spar line and Thomas turns his head.

I don't look to see which cadet has fallen. I don't have to. It makes no difference.

Energy shifts within the arena. Cadets slow, swing their spathas at half pace. Thomas drops his guard, assumes the drill is over. Too bad for him. Master Trainer Cassian hasn't ordered a stop to the drill, so I raise my sword and keep going.

"Jupiter strike you, Matthias!" Thomas blocks my shoulder blow with the edge of his spatha, then swoops it down to my calf. I deflect the counterstrike easily.

"Don't let the priest hear you. He'll think you're a pagan."

Thomas glances at the trainers, who are busy with the fallen cadet, then lets out another pagan curse under his faltering breath.

"You're slower than a drunken snail," I say, though Thomas is faster than me. "You think you'll survive initiation moving like that?"

Thomas uses his height to intimidate. "Get off my back. You're like a rash, weasel." He thrusts forward and catches a piece of my tunic.

"That's better." I dodge, try not to laugh and fail.

Thomas springs again.

"Halt." Lev orders us to attention before Thomas can land a satisfying blow.

Thomas spits phlegm onto the dirt of the arena floor, kisses the small stone cross hanging around his neck, then punches me in the arm.

I smile up at him. "Better luck next round."

We separate from our opponents and return to our lines, shoulders pressed back, arms at our sides, spathas in our right hands, points down. Chests heave. We exhale through our mouths. Puffs of white float upward.

Master Trainer Cassian bends to inspect the fallen boy. It's Regius, thick-limbed, strong-bodied, weak-spleened. He should have washed out of the academy last year, but numbers are down.

When the master trainer rises, he nods to the two closest cadets. Without a word they pick Regius up roughly, one at each shoulder, and half walk, half drag their classmate out the west gate. Unlike the fallen youngster, Regius doesn't resist.

"Juniors, forward," Master Trainer Cassian says.

Thomas and I, along with the other twenty-two junior cadets, separate ourselves from the seniors to stand shoulder to shoulder in front of the master trainer. The seniors remain in their drill lines behind us.

The master trainer lets us wait at attention. He crosses his massive arms, bends his head and listens to his assistant trainers. First Fabius, recently assigned to our garrison, then Levius.

I give Thomas an almost imperceptible nudge with my elbow. Thomas doesn't move. Doesn't smile. He looks straight ahead, his chest still heaving.

"Thomas," the master trainer calls.

"Yes, sir."

"Step back in the drill line."

Thomas returns to his place among the seniors.

I suppress a smile. My turn will come by summer.

Despite the cold, sweat runs from my armpit down my ribs tickling my side. I ignore it. I don't allow myself to adjust my boot, which has folded at the heel. Master Trainer Cassian is watching. Lev and Fabius, too. I move my attention outside my body as if the discomfort were happening to someone else. The juniors are moments from a dismissal. Soon we'll be in the thermae, warm and scrubbed. I can adjust and scratch then.

"Matthias."

I lift my chin. "Yes, sir."

"Back in line."

My thoughts race. My blood pumps. Was this it? My turn, too? Three months early. An honor. I return to the drill line to stand next to Thomas. I resist the urge to look up at my friend or over at the trainers.

Don't serve yourself a feast when there's no food on the table—my father's voice again.

Calm down. With Thomas, there are fifteen senior cadets. I'm probably staying to even the number.

Or to make Thomas look good, another familiar voice forces its way up from the grave. *You owe a debt, little brother. Remember? Tiews has been waiting to collect it. It could be today.*

I can't look back into shadows now. Can't let old ghosts cripple me, whatever is to come.

I steady my mind.

"Front line, dismissed," Lev says. The junior class marches out the west gate in single file behind Fabius, leaving the older cadets alone in the arena.

Unfed and worn down, those that remain wait for the next command.

Thomas leans forward as if ready to sprint out of the gate behind his old class. His breath is clipped and shallow. If he doesn't calm down, conserve his energy, the dumb-arse will drop in two rounds.

I forget my own pumping blood. I want to shove Thomas, tell him to stop burning fuel, but the master trainer stands front and center, his burly shadow looming over us.

I hold my head still, let go of nagging voices and thoughts of Thomas and focus directly ahead, staring into the master trainer's center mass.

"Seniors," Master Trainer Cassian says, and I hear the word as if the master trainer is speaking to me alone. "Same promise. Training continues until the first of you earns a ticket to the Greek. Face off."

The Hound of Hel,
A Trickster's spawn,
Escapes his chains,
Ransacks the dawn.

Oaths forsaken,
Son slashes son,
The Hound of Hel,
Is free to run.*

Inspired by Verse 58 of the Poetic Edda - Volopso

THE ANGEL OF DEATH

A GIRL SHOULD HAVE BEEN HOLDING the sacrificial stone. Not me. *A girl.* But the Angel of Death was losing her vision.

I shifted my weight. The smooth, flat stone—two fingers thick, two feet wide across the top—teetered on my outstretched arms, a wolf's face carved into its surface. The morning was damp, the stone plate heavy and slick. A gnat danced in front of my eyes, then flew up my nose. No amount of wiggling satisfied the itch. Under my breath, I cursed my wild, red mane of hair, swearing a silent oath to shave my head by sunset.

Beside me, the Angel of Death lifted her ragged face to the dawn. Her claw-like fingers clutched a plump, live raven in one hand, a dagger in the other.

She raised the sacrifice to the Greuthungi clans first—to the forest clans and the hill clans and finally to the royal clan of Amal, my clan—then beckoned to Dagmar the Younger, the thirteen-year-old son of our dead Amal leader.

Dagmar knelt before the Angel, the Council of

Greuthungi Elders behind him. The priestess touched the flat end of her blade to the prince's forehead, to single him out so Tiews would know him.

Someday Prince Dagmar would lead all the Greuthungi, uniting those of us who lived within Roman territory with the free clans north of the Great Donau River. Together we would carve out *Gothia*, a land of our own. It had been read.

Next, the Angel turned toward the Tervingi and to Helmreik the One-Eyed, headman of the Balthi clan. Helmreik's two remaining sons flanked him.

The Balthi called themselves royal, too, but I was sure this was a lie.

Helmreik had a thick neck, broad shoulders and a swollen gut protruding out over his belt. He wore a permanent scowl and a leather patch where his right eye used to be. When he bent his head—enough to fulfill his duty, but no more—the Tervingi clans bowed, too.

Behind Dagmar and Helmreik, the many clans of the two rivers had gathered—as they did every year for the offering —in the sacred meadow, surrounded by the rune-carved pines of Hel's Forest. After midday, all the Goths— Greuthungi and Tervingi—would leave the field, feast for three days, talk of lands and rights and marriages and their mutual hate of the Romans, and go back to baiting and fighting and sometimes killing each other.

For now, the two sides stood close together, too close, almost a single mass. I watched the dung-haired, thick-middled Tervingi clans with suspicion.

At the center of the circle, the Angel uttered ancient words to the goddess Nerthus for a plentiful harvest. If pleased with the offering, Nerthus would watch over the reaping, the mothers and the hearths. Clansmen chanted in turn. Eldermen thumped walking sticks against soft earth to the rhythm of the words.

I shifted again. I had to piss.

The Angel called to Tiews. No ritual ended without paying tribute to the bloody, one-armed master, for justice and for strength in battle.

What battle? I sulked. The crowd was mostly children, women and old men. *None of you do the fighting. You're farmers.*

I willed the Angel to speak faster.

WHEN SHE HAD ARRIVED the evening before on her proud white mare—her apprentice clearing the path in front of her—the Angel of Death ordered all the girls between eight summers and ten to the open space between the longhouses.

A pack of willing lasses formed a line. I, being *a boy*, was not in this line.

Ermalinde, Prince Dagmar's youngest sister, pressed her way to the front and jostled for position. When it was her turn to be considered, the Angel bent close and peered at the princess, frowned, then made her way down the line.

Ermi looked like she wanted to throw something at the priestess to get her attention, make the elder woman turn around and pick her. But the Angel moved on and freckle-faced Ermi had to stand there and be silent.

I laughed and stuck my tongue out at her.

Ermi would come after me when Alma the Witch let her loose, but for now, she couldn't make a noise. I prepared to milk every drop from the situation, except the Angel had finished her inspection of the eligible girls and was roving through the earnest mothers who pushed their older and younger daughters forward.

To my horror, the high priestess pointed beyond the cluster to where I stood.

"That one," she said, "the red one."

I heard a burst of laughter from the crowd, cut short, followed by strangled snickers.

The older boys marshaled behind the clan elders and blew kisses at me, my brother out in front. Big surprise. Karig was always out in front. And our cousin Keldamar was there. And Dagmar, too.

Her choice made, the Angel allowed herself to be wrapped in deer hide and led to a bench near a fire. Her apprentice—a stick-thin Tervingi girl about Karig's age—remained by her side.

I opened my mouth to protest. My mother shut it for me. She had me in her iron grip before I could charge after the hecklers. Then she manhandled me into our family long-house and calmly threatened to shorten my life should I show the Angel a syllable of disrespect.

Next morning, squirming to make it as difficult as possible for my mother to wrangle me into the white linen tunic and sheer undergarment, I pleaded, I argued, I even spat.

"It's 'cause of my stupid hair."

"Raise your arm."

"Tiews will know I'm not a girl. He'll curse us for sure."

"Hold still."

"I won't." I stomped, startling the goat and chickens. My

mother might kill me, but my life would be over if I stepped out of the longhouse with a rose embroidered sash around my waist and lavender autumn Crocus in my hair.

The sting of her wooden spoon barely registered.

I might have said more, but Uncle Adalgar appeared in the doorway. "Obey your mother," he said, ending the fight.

Scars ran up and down Adalgar's bare arms, along his neck, into the gray of his red beard. If I stood on top of the side table, I'd still be too short to look my uncle in the eye. "Yes, sir," I said.

My mother tossed her spoon lightly on the nearest sleeping rack, drew herself up, and brushed a wayward auburn lock from her face. She let go of my arm and crossed to Adalgar. "Any sign of them?" she said softly.

"None. The road is clear." Adalgar moved further into the open center of the longhouse. "They're not coming."

"And you're sure Gaius received the message?"

Who was Gaius? I didn't dare interrupt to ask.

"I'm not sure of anything. Your average Roman is a lying, two-faced coward. It was a bad idea."

"Sakarig's idea," my mother snapped, then glanced at the door as if someone might be listening.

"That doesn't make it any better." Adalgar reached for the water bucket on the floor next to a support post and raised it to his lips. When he finished drinking, he let water drip from his beard down the front of him. "But my brother is right about one thing." He grimaced. "Helmreik is hungry and bitter and he has the numbers now. A lot of dirt eaters have crossed that river in the last few years.

"The flatland clans and the river clans can't agree on the color of a mud, but I saw them bunched together like old ladies outside the barn yesterday. Helmreik was at the center of it. Only a matter of time before they find a reason to start a fight."

My mother tossed feed to the chickens. "Helmreik can't do anything so long as the Angel watches. He won't risk the runes turning against him." She nodded for emphasis but didn't sound like she believed her own words.

"Hmmph. Helmreik thinks he is a god." Adalgar kissed the arrow of Tiews hanging from a leather strap around his neck. "And he's just lost a son."

"Blood for blood," my mother said. She looked at me, then up to Adalgar. "Pray for Gaius to come today. It has to be today or the Angel won't matter; blood will spill by the end of the feast. I can feel it. Hel whispers in my ear."

"It's out of our hands, Fenja."

To me, Adalgar said, "Get on with it, boy." And he stepped out into the predawn morning.

My mother peered out the door after him. For a moment, she looked old and worried, but when she turned back to me, any sign of disquiet was gone. "You are old enough to dress yourself," she said. "If you are not outside by the start of the procession, I will inform your father when he is next home. You can give him your reasons, but I doubt he'll judge in your favor."

She left me to think over what I'd heard, to punch at a hay mattress, to curse dead ancestors, and to tie the rose sash as neatly as I could manage around my waist.

I didn't drop dead from embarrassment when I stepped from the longhouse.

The Angel waited. Behind her, the Northland clans. All of them. The Greuthungi clans and the Tervingi. More bodies than the open spaces between our Amal longhouses could hold. They overflowed as far as the horse stables, two hundred paces east, where the men disarmed and presented their weapons for storage.

No one entered the sacred place with a weapon.

My mother led me to stand in front of the Angel and held me in place so the old woman's watery eyes and bony fingers could inspect me.

Not even Karig dared break the quiet.

The priestess smacked her lips, motioned to her apprentice and turned her back to me.

The apprentice placed the sacrificial stone plate across my arms. As she adjusted the plate for balance, the girl's unearthly green eyes glowered at me, a churning hatred masked by mouse-brown hair.

The look caught me by surprise. Contempt smothered me like heavy earth. I didn't understand. I rocked back on my heels involuntarily, unable to break eye contact until the girl finished with the stone and returned to the Angel's side.

The apprentice took hold of the Angel's arm to guide the hunched priestess through the wheat field to the trees, murmuring low into the old woman's ear as they walked, with me and the goth clans following behind.

I THOUGHT the worst was over, but once in the meadow, the orders to stand still and hold a plate were proving more challenging than I would have imagined. The need to piss grew desperate. I still had a gnat lodged in my nose and an unbearable itch pestered the bottom of my right foot. Sliding my foot around my sandal made no difference. Frustrated, I peeked down through the space between the stone plate and my body.

My elbow nudged the Angel. She stumbled over a word.

In the endless silence, I dared not look up to see the Angel's expression, but I could see my mother's. From her place in the circle, she pursed her lips and a single, telltale crease appeared above one eye. I froze, my foot half raised. My backside twitched. Gingerly, I lowered my foot and my head.

The Angel resumed her prayers, raising her voice and her arms, phlegm rumbling in her throat. Trance-like, she swayed, the raven trapped in her hand. The doomed bird squawked twice, wriggling until the Angel swiped the knife cleanly across the back of its neck.

I heard a snapping of tiny bones and looked up just in time for entrails to miss the top of my head and splat across the stone plate, over the wolf's face. The Angel ran a long fingernail through the guts. Blood trickled into the carved stone grooves, pooling along the eyes and teeth. The wolf's face turned a dirty red.

Strands of the Angel's gray hair tickled my nose as she leaned over to read the future in the slimy mess. Her breath stank of rotting lettuce, and my stomach churned from the smell of her. If I wasn't allowed to head to the trees soon, I'd pee down my own leg. I closed my eyes.

"Nerthus, Goddess of Earth, grants us a plentiful..." the Angel began, but whatever she would have said next was interrupted when drops of her spittle landed on my cheek.

I shuddered.

The plate slipped one way, then the other, pausing for a

hope-filled blink of an eye before I lost control of it. The plate fell. Instead of soft, late summer grass, it hit a rock and cracked down the middle between the wolf's red-rimmed eyes. The raven's innards—and the fortune to come—oozed through the crack into the ground.

MATHILDE

SILENCE.

A low growl gurgled up from the Angel's throat. Her cloudy eyes shifted from the sunken prophecy to me.

She would curse me. I knew it, and I took to my heels, dodging through an opening in the crowd. A hand grabbed for me and caught hold of my fine linen tunic. I spun out of the grip, lifted the ankle-length fabric above my leggings so it didn't trip me up and sprinted across the meadow for the safety of the trees.

Of course, my mother would send Karig after me. That meant Keldamar, too. Big thugs. Not for the first time, I wished there was another boy my age among the Amal long-houses. Someone who would be on my side. But there were only older boys and elders and toddlers and girls. Girls everywhere.

I was well into the pines before the open spaces narrowed and late summer brush slowed me down, limiting the directions in which I could run. The hem of the tunic snagged on sticker weeds when I let the skirts fall to the ground, so I untied the sash, pulled the tunic and undergarment over my head and threw the cursed material as far as I could.

Bare-chested, I turned south, deeper into the woods.

Grenz Creek gurgled ahead, the boundary of my known world. The Romans—and the gods—had given the Greuthungi clans the lands north of the Grenz. The elders called anything south of the creek the *Verbode*—The Forbidden.

The Verbode was Hel's domain, a vast forest. A skilled man needed five days to travel through the heart of it from north to south before he came out the other side, or so I'd been told. That's if the forest didn't swallow the traveler up. There were specters and bears, monsters and wolves and only a fool would tempt the gods by venturing beyond the Grenz, to where the trees grew thick enough to block out natural light.

I kicked at a pine cone and plotted my next move, considering and discounting hiding places as I went. The women who had gathered fuel all summer had stripped much of the green from shrubs and the under-branches off the trees, leaving only skeletons, none dense enough to conceal me.

I neared the creek and scanned the terrain across the bank.

Good cover along the opposite side.

It would be an easy jump.

I took care of my bladder and calculated the risk I was about to take.

Stupid to think of crossing. Hel would curse me. My children and grandchildren, too. Her breath chilled the back of my neck, and wolf eyes glowed from somewhere in the shadows.

Behind me, I heard the older boys. They had found my trail, and maybe lost it again, and split up to hunt me as they would hunt a wild pig. I could never outrun them. My brother and Keld were twelve—four years older than me— fast and smart and lean and strong and wicked accurate when they threw anything. To get caught would mean a beating for sure, maybe two, and a meeting with the Angel.

But I'd bet my prized hunting knife Karig wouldn't cross the creek into the Verbode. And if Karig didn't dare, Keld wouldn't either. I didn't have to go far into the unknown. Only a few feet. After that, all I'd have to do was wait. Let them grow bored and hungry.

I shuffled my way to the edge of the Grenz, braced myself and leapt to the other side. My knees buckled, but I regained my balance. I took three more terrified steps into the mystic Verbode and—when Hel didn't strike me down— scurried beneath an elderberry bush.

I caught glimpses of movement between the trees. Birds at first, then Karig, nearly silent, leading the way. I paused my breath so I could listen for Keld, who would be somewhere to Karig's right.

The older boys thought they were so clever, crouched and stealthy, with their hand signals and superior tracking skills. They reached the creek downstream of me and crept along the bank edge, scanning for spoor within their familiar hunting grounds.

Neither of them thought to look across the water to my elderberry bush.

Slowly, they edged past me, heading upstream, and I covered my mouth to keep my urge to laugh from giving me away.

Twenty more paces and Karig swiped at a sapling and stood up straight.

"This is stupid." He scowled. "The little turd knows we're here. He's dug in somewhere. Be easier to tease out a pine vole."

"Good point." Keld straightened, too. He was the same height as Karig, the same frame, slightly thinner. Keld could keep up with Karig, and the two were rarely apart. Twins, the elders called them. The difference was in the face, in the eyes. Keld's eyes danced. His lips twitched, even when he tried to be serious, like a joke was ready to roll off his tongue.

Karig was nicer when Keld was around, as if he needed Keld to help him laugh, to help temper the iron that made up Karig's core.

"So what happens if we *do* find him?" Keld pulled a thick, straight stick from the brush and knocked it against a tree trunk to shake the dirt free. He swiped the stick through the air like it was his father's spatha.

I suppressed another giggle.

"You mean after I beat him silly?"

"Yeah, after that."

"He'll get stuffed back into that dress…"

"Some fresh flowers for his hair…"

"And get the lashing of his life after the feast, probably." A branch snapped in the distance and Karig whipped around.

Still. Alert. He scanned the trees, then frowned. "This is stupid," he said again.

I watched them with a sense of victory.

Keld swiped his branch again, then threw it down the creek bank. "Too bad. He looked so pretty dressed like a girl."

"Little Mathilde," Karig said, and the boys looked at each other.

"Mathilde!" they called at the same time and laughed.

"Come on out, little flower."

I didn't want to care, but I did. I felt my face flush hot.

"Mathilde," they took turns singing it in high pitch. Karig doubled over, barely able to breathe, "Mathilde."

Stop laughing!

"Mathilde. Mathilde."

Before I knew what my legs were doing, they had carried me out into the open, across the creek, through the trees and brush. I tackled my brother, pushing him hard in the small of the back. My arms wrapped around my brother's thigh, taking us both down.

When we hit the ground, I scrambled like a madman away from Karig's thrashing legs, rolled to my feet and ran for my life over the uneven ground to reach the edge of the forest before my brother could catch me and beat the life out of me. Instinct propelled me toward our longhouses. What I would do after that, I didn't know. Get my knife. Hide. Run. Keep running.

Karig hissed curses between breaths close behind me. Closer. The ground leveled thirty paces away from the creek, less brush, more space between the trees. Running became easier…for both of us.

My brother's hand locked around my shoulder, pulling me down backward, so I hit the floor of the forest hard with my brother quickly on top of me.

"Hold still."

I kicked my legs, arched my back.

"Stop squirming, and I'll let go." Karig was smiling, enjoying himself.

I didn't stop. I grabbed for Karig's face but couldn't reach that high. His metal rune—the arrow of Tiews, Karig's prize possession—dangled from a leather strap a foot from my nose. I wrapped my fingers around the leather and yanked as hard as I could. The string snapped, leaving two burn marks on either side of Karig's neck and the rune in my hand.

My brother stopped smiling.

With no warning, Karig smashed his forehead into my cheek and rolled me over into a headlock before my head had stopped ringing.

"Give it back to him, Matthi," Keld said. "Karig, that's enough."

Out of the corner of my eye, in a dizzy haze, I saw movement. A figure slipped behind a tree. "Wait…"

"You wanna stop now?" Karig tightened his grip around my neck. "You want mercy? Little Mathilde's scared? Little Mathilde's gonna get a beating."

"Someone's…coming…" I squirmed in Karig's grip. I needed to speak but couldn't get the words out. My sore cheek pulsed with the pressure in my head. I kicked harder, tried to yell, and only choked. The trees faded to black.

"Ow!" Karig flinched. His grip loosened. "Ow!" He flinched again. "What the…"

"You let him go, Karig." It was a girl's voice. Prince Dagmar's sister, Ermalinde, the freckled princess.

Through the black, I heard another thump.

"Ow." Karig released me, shoved me away and jumped to his feet.

I heaved in a breath, coughed. My world came back into focus, Karig's rune still in my hand. I wrapped the leather strap around my wrist and tied the loose ends, tightening them with my teeth. The metal dangled against the back of my hand.

Now, I had something to trade.

"Aunt Brunehild's going to tan your hide, Ermi. Get back to the gathering." Karig shooed her away.

Standing ten paces away with a handful of pebbles, Ermalinde stuck out her chin. She chucked another fig-sized stone at Karig, pelting him in the chest.

"Knock it off. You think I won't hit a girl?" Karig lunged at her, a scare tactic.

She didn't budge.

"Try it. It'll be really embarrassing when you lose." She was half Karig's size, three years younger, and dead serious.

Karig threw up his hands.

Keld laughed. "You're all honey and goose down, Ermi. Make a sweet, biddable bride someday."

Ermi threw a pebble at Keld's nose. Keld dodged, and it nicked the side of his head.

"No weapons, Ermi." Karig lunged again, this time for real. He caught her wrist and tried to pry the pebbles from her fingers.

She yanked her hand away. "We're not in the meadow."

"Lucky she couldn't bring her sling." Keld rubbed his temple.

I made it to my feet and wanted to run again, not from a wolf this time, or my brother, but from the humiliation of having been saved by a girl.

Ermalinde clearly had more to say, but Karig shushed her.

He paused. Listened. He picked up two of the bigger stones that had struck him.

"Show yourself, dirt eater," he said to the trees.

A sturdy, thin-lipped boy emerged from behind a pine and faced us with his empty hands resting at his sides.

"Leogern." Karig kept the stones raised. "Where are the others?"

Leogern was the youngest son of Helmreik the One-Eyed. A Balthi, so the Tervingi called Leogern a prince. To me, he was a walking tree trunk and seemed about that smart. Leogern was two years younger than Karig but almost as big. He shrugged his broad shoulders and stared at Karig without answering.

Keld moved in front of Ermalinde. "Stay behind me."

Ermi stepped to one side to see.

Karig listened to the forest. "You lost?"

Leogern shook his head.

A moment later, a sharp voice sliced through the trees. "Leogern!"

The young Balthi stiffened, then bolted. His gorilla of an older brother, Tanfrid—nearly the age to join the auxiliary— crunched through pine needles with no attempt at stealth. His cousin, Fredo, and two of the oldest boys from their Balthi clan fanned out, blocking the way back to the Angel.

"Useless as a fart," Tanfrid said as Leogern shot passed him.

Tanfrid tilted his head to one side and looked past Karig at me. He was as thick as his brother only taller, a brick for a head, the top of his ears puffed out from fighting.

"You stepped in a steaming pile of cow dung, didn't you?" Tanfrid bared his teeth at me, many cracked or missing, his eyes half-mast. "This might be the best day of my life."

THE BALTHI

THE FOUR BALTHI came at us. Tanfrid led with his cousin Fredo on his left side. On his right was a lumbering giant and a smaller, smooth-faced blond boy.

I backed up, prepared to run then looked to Karig. My brother planted his feet, stuck out his chest and waited for Tanfrid to meet us, so I held my ground, too.

The white sacrificial tunic hung from Tanfrid's belt.

"Come on, you clumsy runt," he said. "The priestess is waiting."

I glared at the tunic. "No," I said. "They can get a girl to hold the sacrifice."

"They wouldn't trust you to wipe a donkey's backside now," Tanfrid said slowly as if I were a toddler. "Move your feet."

Hel's breath fell on the back of my neck a second time, and I gripped Karig's rune—still twisted around my left hand—for courage.

Karig, who moments before had been choking the life out

of me, moved to shield me. "If he's no longer trusted, then he's no longer needed. Why would a *prince* come to fetch him?"

The Balthi was sizing up my brother with a heavy-lidded gaze. "You think the gods will be satisfied with a mangy bird after such an insult? They will demand blood, the blood of the offender."

Karig scoffed. "The Angel would not sacrifice a son of Sakarig."

I believed Tanfrid. I had messed up, perhaps angered the gods against the Goths and proven myself unworthy. I would have to face the consequences. Still, as ashamed as I was, there was no way I was walking out of the forest under Tanfrid's thuggish control.

Keld moved from Ermi to stand with Karig, forming a human wall in front of me.

Ermi followed. "It is not for a dirt eater to lay hands on a Greuthung," she said, but no one acknowledged she had spoken.

Tanfrid's dead eyes came to life. He closed the distance between him and Karig. "You're not above the justice of the gods? Your father's no king, no reiks. He's a fill-in. And it's time Sakarig learns what it is to lose something," Tanfrid smiled. He bent his head and crooned to Karig. "It'd be so much better if it was you."

I knew what was coming. Tanfrid was after a fight. And my brother wouldn't back down. I broke away from the others and turned, sprinting as fast as the uneven ground and brush would allow toward the *Verbode*.

"Don't stop," my brother called.

"The sons of Sakarig have no honor," Tanfrid shouted after me.

But I did stop. I reached the spot where Keld had thrown the long stick, retrieved it from the bank of the Grenz and scooped up a short but sturdy piece of wood for my other hand, then reversed my course in time to see Karig lunge toward the Balthi prince.

Tanfrid's hand disappeared inside his tunic.

"No!" I shouted uselessly.

My brother would never believe another Goth, even a Terving, would break the sacred rules, so Karig was still moving forward when Tanfrid drew out a knife, which Tanfrid's broad leather belt had kept hidden. The Balthi prince took a swipe at Karig. It was a defensive move, more to startle than to cut.

"I'm not supposed to kill you. My father has forbidden it." Tanfrid sliced again through the air, manipulating Karig backward as Fredo closed in on Karig's right. "But I swear before Tiews; I will return successful from this hunt."

The third Balthi, tallest of the four, moved in on the other side of the group and braced Keld, while the youngest of Tanfrid's clansmen—a blond boy who looked more Greuthung than Terving—broke off to come after me. Like a bull, I charged at him, dodging at the last moment.

"You had a blade within the sacred place?" Ermalinde admonished. "Who is offending the gods now?"

Tanfrid ignored her.

She threw a stone. It only bounced off Tanfrid's thick frame.

Karig spun to one side out of Tanfrid's reach, too close to Fredo, who got hold of Karig's arm. Fredo managed to gain control over my brother's other arm, then held him while Tanfrid landed a solid punch to Karig's chin.

I heard the terrible crunch of bone against bone.

Karig's head wobbled from the impact. He kicked out wildly at Tanfrid, catching the Balthi's upper thigh, just south of Tanfrid's groin. Angered, Tanfrid delivered a hard blow to Karig's ribs.

Karig dropped to his knees.

"Karig!" I yelled.

Keld struggled against the taller, bigger third Balthi.

The blond angled to cut me off from the others. I slipped through an open space between my attacker and an overgrown fern, and charged, sticks in hand, at Fredo who had lifted Karig from the ground by his armpits.

I was within ten paces when the blond caught up with me. He wrapped a hand around my face from behind, straining my neck and stopping my forward progress. The hand slid down to my mouth, and I bit it hard. The blond squealed and let go.

The path was clear now.

Karig had regained his senses enough to slam his body against Fredo.

While Fredo struggled, Tanfrid stepped in front of his cousin to meet me, knife in hand. I slid to a stop a few paces away, glaring at Tanfrid and the knife.

"No one will give a rabbit turd if you're bleeding, so long as I get you back to the Angel," he said.

I wasn't listening. I had my plan, and my courage, and rushed forward. Tanfrid raised his arm to block a blow from the long stick, but at the last moment, I lowered the stick to waist level and shoved it past Tanfrid and into Karig's hand.

Karig grabbed hold.

I rammed the small stick as hard as I could into Tanfrid's gut. It was not graceful, but it stunned the dirt-eating prince, and I was several paces away before Tanfrid could react. Dodging the blond again, I found open space.

Karig had used the end of his stick to jab Fredo firmly in the ribs. An awkward strike, but enough for Fredo to lose his hold. Karig slipped out of his grasp and swung the stick against the side of Fredo's head. Without pausing, Karig spun around, swept the stick up, and struck Tanfrid hard under the chin.

Tanfrid stumbled.

Fredo cursed, holding his head. Red trickled out of his ear between his fingers.

"Run," Karig yelled.

But the third Terving had a grip on a mass of Keld's thick, sandy hair. When Karig turned to go after Keld's attacker, Tanfrid caught Karig around the neck from behind and forced him to the ground, knocking the wind out of him. Tanfrid reached down, pulled Karig up by the tunic and pressed his blade tight under Karig's chin.

Fredo continued to hold his ear with one hand. He grabbed Ermalinde with the other. Ermi tried to bite him. She wiggled this way and that. Fredo didn't look at her. His dung-brown eyes never left Karig.

"Let them go," I said stupidly, staying out of the blond's reach.

"Come with me, and I will release them," Tanfrid said. His chin had already begun to swell. "That, or I'll slit your brother's throat."

"You wouldn't dare!" Ermi screamed. Fredo wrenched her arm back to get a better grip, and she screamed again.

Keld stopped struggling. He was studying Tanfrid and looked afraid. "Quiet, Ermi," he said.

"Look at that," Tanfrid sneered, his expression cold, merciless. "A smart pebble head." To me, he said, "There will be blood offered today. The gods will have yours, or I will have your brothers."

I looked at the clansmen, at Karig, behind me toward our longhouses and then through the trees to the sacred place. I didn't know what to do.

Karig shook his head, tried to speak, but hadn't regained his breath. The words wouldn't come.

I dropped my stick. "Let him go," I said again.

The blond waited for Tanfrid's order.

Tanfrid let go of Karig, then signaled a release of Keld and Ermalinde.

I tugged on the leather strap of the rune and unwrapped it from around my wrist. I crossed to Tanfrid and dropped the rune beside my brother as I passed.

The three Greuthungi—my family—were left to pick themselves up off the forest floor as Tanfrid led me back to the Angel of Death.

THE GARRISON

355 AD

SENIORS

Tenth hour.

We're still in the arena, empty except for the senior cadets, the master trainer and Assistant Trainer Levius.

I may be here to even the numbers, but the trainers have pushed me as hard as Thomas. Harder. I'm in this to promote until the master trainer tells me otherwise.

Training has narrowed to one drill, the same drill, performed again and again.

Seniors stand in two lines, each facing a sparring partner. Assistant Trainer Levius calls an opening strike. The lines take turns attacking and defending. We play out the opening strike and free spar until told to stop. Sometimes that's three moves, sometimes fifty, we move each other in and out of the late afternoon sunlight, searching for an advantage until shadow covers all but the top rows of the arena's eastern seating.

Every ten drills, we break for water.

I've kept count of the number of drills—the number of

strikes within each drill—between water breaks. It's kept my mind off the blister on my ankle and the raw bite of my palms which are a thin skin layer away from bleeding. After an hour at the same monotonous sequence, my focus is cracking. I begin to lose count.

A body hits the dirt down the line. Thomas turns his head toward the thud. Hope bubbles up against my will. Perhaps the day is over. I force myself not to look.

Eat from the plate in front of you.

Master Trainer Cassian has preached those words every day of the six years I've spent inside these garrison walls. My father said them, too. And they are right. Fate will decide if the fallen cadet rises or stays down. To hope for an outcome won't make it so. It saps energy to dream of food when there is none or to think of quitting when that isn't an option. Hope can mess with a soldier's head, lead him to focus on what isn't there, lure him into fighting himself.

Mostly I'm fine. I can still raise my sword arm to strike. My legs are holding strong. That's all I need to know. I move toward Thomas.

"Stop," Lev says. We lower our spathas—eight pairs of cadets—and step away from our opponents.

The fallen cadet must have regained his feet. Thomas turns back to me, eyes unfocused, shoulders slumped. A streak of soot runs along his hairline from forehead to chin.

Lev calls the next opening strike. "*Humilis ictu.*" A low thrust.

Thomas steps with his left foot and thrust the tip of his spatha at my thigh. I parry, offer a counter blow. Swords knock against wooden shields in free spar. Dull thuds. The strikes have lost force, but we keep going.

"Stop," Lev says.

A pause for five breaths.

"Again."

Thomas stumbles, coughs, drops his shield mid-drill, bends to retrieve it. He looks up at me, defenseless.

I tap him with the edge of my foot. "Get moving, lazy-arse." Neither of us is laughing now.

Thomas shakes his head. "I'm finished, Matthias."

To our left a droop-eyed, pock-marked, rabble-rouser called Blasius, snorts and swings hard at his sparring partner, Lastimus. Blasius has the lean muscle and the stink of a full-grown man. Lastimus is a hand-width shorter, a hard and wiry jackal with a crooked smile twisted into a smirk.

Thomas rises, leans to one side, rubs his thigh like it's cramping, bends forward again and moans. Any moment Thomas will call it quits. He may have done enough to promote but to advertise weakness is to open a fresh wound and call the dogs. Blasius and Lastimus have been showing signs of fatigue. Now they smell blood.

"I can't do this," Thomas says. His eyes water.

I slam my body into my friend, willing the stupid-arse to sew his yap closed.

Thomas keeps his legs, but barely. He shoves me back. "What are you trying to prove?"

I shift my eyes to the older cadets and give Thomas a meaningful look. Thomas glances at Blasius, then at Jason the Beardless and No-Neck Nonius on our right. Our new comrades. Our new adversaries. Thomas draws his mouth into a thin line and continues the drill in silence.

Water break, no sitting.

I gulp down as much as I can before Blasius knocks me out of the way. I take a place in the inspection line and wait for Thomas, who is taking his time at the fountain's edge. Thomas sways a bit from side to side.

Leave him be. The long-absent voice—Karig's voice—cuts through my thoughts. *His battle is none of your business, little brother.*

I rub my face, clear my head, then drop my eyes and let Thomas go. Just as well I start thinking of my own situation.

Motionless, the cold attacks. My muscles stiffen.

Cato shuffles up on my right, eyes and mouth drawn down in a sleepy pout. Blasius takes position on my other side.

Great.

"This is so unfair," Cato whines to the sky. "Someone is due the lash after this. No food, working us to death. My father will hear about this."

He needs to shut up.

When Cato turns to me, I lean away and brush against Blasius, who shoves me.

"You still here, dirt eater?" Blasius doesn't bother to lower his voice.

The trainers are several paces away, but close enough to issue demerits if they choose to pay attention.

"Just warming up," I say through my teeth.

"No." Blasius leans down close enough for me to smell stale garlic on his breath. "You're gonna quit so we can hit the baths."

"Why? You getting tired?"

Lastimus takes position on the other side of Blasius, his

mouth still twisted in a smirk. "You've offended him, Blasius. Matthias is no dirt eater."

Blasius raises an eyebrow in mock surprise. "No?"

"No, dirt eaters are the farmer kind of savages. I mean, they're all farmers now, but, you know, dirt eaters are the ones with the dingy hair? Our boy Matthias is the other kind. The piss-haired kind. The ones who used to chase after their food. He's a pebble head. Isn't that right, Matthias?" Lastimus tilts his head to see around Blasius, all innocence and goodwill.

Insults aside, what Lastimus says is true. I hold steady.

"No way. This kid's not a tow-head. Look at him." Blasius flicked the back of my scalp, which is shaded red with two weeks of growth.

I swat the senior's hand away. Blasius laughs.

"He looks like his mother. Half dirt, half stone." Lastimus smiles like he's preparing for a punchline. "But you know what they say about half-breeds…?"

I *do* know what they say about half-breeds. And now I can't help myself. I grip my shield, ready to shut Lastimus up with the edge of it.

At the same moment, Lev calls the inspection line to attention. Like a trained dog, I freeze mid-motion and straighten.

Lastimus and Blasius bridle their sniggers and come to attention, too.

Master Trainer Cassian takes one end of our line, Lev the other. They work their way toward the middle.

I wait for my turn, thrown off balance, willing my breath to slow, my jaw muscles to relax. It's been a while since another cadet dared bait me. I'd have made short work of any junior who got in my face like that. As a junior I'm one of the oldest, the most experienced, a lead cadet. I've earned my place and the respect that goes with it. But Blasius and Lastimus have sent a clear message. If I promote, my training stick will be history. I'll go from the highest junior rank to the runt of the senior litter, and life's tough at the bottom.

I look out over the arena, and feel like I'm eight years old. Like when I stepped through the arena gate for the first time, and Karig was nowhere to be seen. That day, the sky had turned black with the promise of a downpour, and I'd ended the training with my face held down in the mud so long I thought I'd never breathe again.

I watch the sky as the trainers close in. It was clear in the morning. Now cloud cover rolls in, dark in patches.

As if he could feel the change in my confidence, Blasius bumps me with his elbow and whispers so only I can hear, "It'll be you that quits first, puppy dog. It's gotta be you."

They are trying to get into my head. Stupid to let them.

The wind picks up, swirling dust. It rips through my tunic and worn leggings as if I were streaking naked across the parade grounds. My body begins to shake.

Lev reaches me. "Chest out," he says, his eyes narrow, deep-set into weathered skin.

Lev speaks and acts like a Roman, but everyone knows he's not, and for an instant, I see the faces of my father and brother in the assistant trainer's white-blond hair and chiseled features. It's the look of the Greuthungi Goth, wild and unyielding as the Steppe from which we came.

Many of the cadets and legionnaires have barbarian features, but Lev is the only other pure-blood Goth inside this elite academy. Here they mold the sons of noblemen and high-ranking legionnaires…and one red-headed barbarian hostage.

Hostage.

The word never felt right. The other cadets think I'm here to ensure my father's loyalty. Maybe that's truth—it's what my brother thought—but I don't think of it that way and never have. I draw myself up and pull my shoulders back.

Lev's just an assistant trainer, but the master trainer listens to him, and that's something. It's enough to remind me I can belong here.

He moves my arm, inspects my hands. A callous on my sword hand has ripped clean off and the new skin, too. Blood streaks my palm. I'm worried he'll send me to the Greek, a good excuse to end the day if the trainers feel the need, but Lev grants me a quick nod and moves on to Blasius.

Moments later, Lev orders us back to the drill lines.

"Double-time. Let's go," the master trainer rasps.

I run, but my foot catches on something, and I pitch forward. My left knee and my bloody right palm scrape along the pebbled dirt.

"As clumsy as your brother, aren't you?" Lastimus says as he passes. "You gonna make a run for it, like he did? Guess he wasn't so tough, in the end."

Blasius knocks into me before I can regain my balance, and my palm scrapes dirt again.

"Is there a problem?" The master trainer asks. The other cadets are in position.

"No, sir," Blasius says.

"No, sir," Lastimus says.

"No, sir." I find my feet, retrieve my spatha and shield, then join the line, knuckles white.

My discipline evaporates. I want to hurt them, swing at a kneecap, limp one of them for life. Karig would have done it. Karig wouldn't have hesitated. But I'm not Karig.

Coward, Karig taunts me.

If I were outside the walls, if this were Greuthungi land...

I haven't allowed myself this kind of thinking in years. I'm tired. The day is getting to me. This isn't the Goth laeti, and Roman cadets don't play by Goth rules.

I shove Karig, the laeti and old memories away. Remember where you are, I tell myself, which usually works to calm me, but I feel like I'm sinking.

I look across the line at Thomas. Thomas looks away. Seniors tower over me to my left and right. Eyes shift in my direction, mouths set in grim resentment.

It has to be you, puppy dog, Blasius said.

He is a loud bully, but that doesn't make him wrong. None of this is about Thomas. If Thomas were the only junior promoting, someone would have earned a ticket by now. Cato, maybe. Or Ionius, he's younger and small. The cadets could say they let the camp prefect's son have his moment. They could call it a duty. But no cadet can afford to fall before a Goth. Roman pride won't stand for it. It isn't Thomas who has to prove himself. The other cadets are waiting for me to quit, wanting it to be the fourteen-year-old barbarian that ends the day's pain.

"South line, shift left," Lev orders.

Thomas avoids eye contact and moves to stand in front of Jason the Beardless. Thomas is standing straighter now. Perhaps he has energy enough for another few rounds.

I look hard at my friend then turn my attention inward. I take inventory of the tools I have left. My arms and legs will last. My wind is stable. If the blister on my foot or the raw of my palms are uncomfortable, well, the cadets around me aren't faring better. Some, like Thomas, are near empty.

Let them sweat. Let them fall, the lot of them.

Thomas too.

Master Trainer Cassian has given me this honor, a full season before my time. The master trainer must think I'm ready, and his is the only opinion that matters. I won't spit on that trust by giving up.

Someday, I'll be a legionnaire. A centurion. It's time to earn my way. Then these slack-jaws can kiss my high ranking backside.

Lastimus shifts from Blasius to stand in front of me. He wears the same twisted smile.

I grind my feet into the dirt of the arena floor and smile back.

GOTH LAETI

Greuthungi Lands - Six Years Earlier

JUSTICE

Tanfrid and the other three Balthi surrounded me, dwarfed me. I didn't consider them.

Somewhere ahead, the Angel of Death waited for me with her knife, and, in my eight-year-old mind, the situation was simple. I had loused up something important and deserved what punishment came to me. I detested Tanfrid, but he wasn't wrong. I needed to make things right with the gods, so I forced one foot in front of the other and kept pace with the big thug and his pack as we approached the edge of the trees.

My bladder was empty, or I may have pissed myself. My lower lip trembled. The effort to still it made my eyes water. A wolf's growl rumbled in my ear, hot breath in the chilled air.

Tanfrid's cousin, Fredo, was sullen. "You shouldn't have brought the knife."

"Shut up," Tanfrid said.

"You risk everything. The gods will turn from us."

Ermalinde had said this, too. I hoped it was true.

Tanfrid looked annoyed, no hint of guilt on his face. He came to a sudden halt and grabbed Fredo by the front of his tunic. "I said shut up."

Fredo pushed Tanfrid away.

Tanfrid let him go. "If I hadn't carried the knife we'd be holding nothing but our manhood right now."

Fredo started walking again. Tanfrid held out a hand to stop him. "Don't you get it? The gods have smiled on us. The brat served himself up. We couldn't have wished for a better opportunity. My father will get his vengeance and the Tervingi men will see that the gods don't favor the Greuthungi anymore."

"But the treaty. We pledged our loyalty to the Greuthungi…"

"We pledged loyalty at the point of a sword. We pledged to Dagmar the Elder. Where is he now? Dead. The gods turned from him." Tanfrid glanced sideways at me and sneered like the sight of me made him sick. "The gods turn from Sakarig now."

I looked from Tanfrid to Fredo, trying to piece together what I was hearing.

Fredo shook his head. "And if the runes say different? The Angel of Death is a Greuthung. He's an Amal. She could send him to hunt a squirrel for his punishment."

"The Angel *was* a Greuthung. Now she is nearly blind, and half her mind is gone. She is what Vigdis says she is."

Vigdis? Who was Vigdis?

Fredo frowned. "Vigdis is just an apprentice."

In my mind, the girl's disturbing green eyes and silent hate bored into me again. I shook her image away.

"You don't get it." Tanfrid leaned in, lowered his voice, like he was about to betray a secret. "The runes speak to Vigdis now. The Angel hears what Vigdis whispers. Vigdis told my father our time is coming, and today she will read in our favor. Then these weak-spleened Tervingi farmers will see that Tervingi fortunes have changed. They will find their courage, rally behind our clan, force Sakarig to hand over control of the auxiliary. Those fat Roman noblemen will have to negotiate with my father and the Tervingi elders then. The Balthi will take what should have belonged to us all along."

I listened, understanding only that the green-eyed apprentice was somehow controlling the Angel, and that Tanfrid and his father were up to no good.

My lip stopped trembling. My fear turned to anger.

"Get moving," Tanfrid snarled at me.

I nearly lost my nerve when Tanfrid pushed me past the rune-carved trees into the sacred meadow.

The crowd was divided into two unequal groups. Helm-reik and the dirt eaters had gathered on one side and filled more than half the open space. Prince Dagmar, the Council of Greuthungi Elders and our Greuthungi clans filled the rest.

Between the two sides, the Angel knelt on an undyed wool blanket. I saw only a lump of white linen with stringy gray hair. The Angel may have been praying, or maybe she napped. Her eyes were closed. Vigdis the Apprentice knelt by the old woman's side, her head bowed. Under her brow, she peered at me, and I feared her strange magic.

There was a smell of danger in the air. Whatever peace had been between the clans was gone. If the clansmen had not presented their weapons at the barn, to face the gods unarmed, blood would have spilled.

"There he is!" came a shout from the Tervingi side when we came into view.

"Tie him to the whipping post!" someone demanded.

I searched our Greuthungi side for my mother and found her standing directly behind Prince Dagmar and the eldermen. A small comfort.

With my head high, I set my course for the Angel's blanket to receive whatever was to come, but Tanfrid seized my shoulder and wrenched me toward his father, Helmreik the One-Eyed, who stood at the front of the Tervingi side. Helmreik had dared position himself closest to the Angel—usually the right of Prince Dagmar—and I wanted to yell at him to move away, to get back where he belonged.

"You've had success," Helmreik said. "Well done."

The Balthi leader took hold of the back of my neck. He wasn't gentle. The headman's fingers dug into my skin, but I refused to cry out.

Hel's Forest beckoned again. It would be nothing to twist from Helmreik's grip. No one except Karig and my father could hold me when I decided on my freedom. But I'd given my word.

Without his word, a man is hollow, my father whispered.

Even though all my father's words were for Karig, I heard them too and carried them in my heart. If I couldn't be trusted to hold a stone plate like any girl in the clan had managed to do, I could stand tall now. Do that right, at least. I let Helmreik keep hold of me, wishing I was as big as Karig so it would mean something if I punched the bloated reiks in his fat belly.

Across the divide, Karig, Keld and Ermalinde squeezed their way through the mass of Greuthungi. My brother wasn't heckling now. He found a place beside our mother, his face marked from the fight. Keld stood next to his siblings and Uncle Adalgar, and Ermalinde took position between Dagmar and Ishild, her older sister.

Clutching me, Helmreik inhaled. "The gods must be satisfied." He belted out the words so the farthest clansmen among us could hear. "Atonement must be made."

"Be easy, all of you." Prince Dagmar called out, his voice high and uncertain. He stepped into the open space between the two sides with three Greuthungi eldermen behind him.

Dagmar sucked in air, his face flushed red. "I've sent men to the Amal farms with orders to return with the fattest of our stock. A goat as white as snow and bulging from the summer."

Helmreik laughed. "A goat did not disrespect the gods. This boy alone is responsible. He must be the one to make amends." Then louder, he said, "Young Prince Dagmar would risk the future of our clans? Why would that be? Is it because he is more afraid of this boy's father than the power of Tiews?"

Murmurs rose up from both sides.

The Greuthungi boys inflated their chest at the smell of an insult.

The Tervingi elders pounded their walking sticks in the soft grass to show support. A gray-haired Tervingi woman near me wrinkled her leathery nose, pursed her dung-eating lips, and glared at me as if she'd cook me for the evening meal if given her way. I looked around me and realized for the first time how many of the Tervingi boys were nearing military age. Many more than on our Greuthungi side. There were full-grown men among them, too. Fighting-aged men. *Why were they here?* They shuffled and shifted, a dangerous energy growing among them. They edged closer to Helmreik, pressing against each other behind Tanfrid, closing the divide between the two Goth sides.

Prince Dagmar raised his arm, but the sticks kept pounding. He raised his changing voice, and it cracked. "Sakarig has led Greuthungi and Tervingi sons alike for fifteen years. He has devoted his life to our people. Now a Tervingi reiks casts a shadow over Sakarig's honor?"

"Sakarig the Noble!" from the Greuthungi side.

"He's more Roman than Goth," said a Terving.

"Sakarig the Roman!" the chant took hold. The Tervingi boys grew restless.

Uncle Adalgar stepped from the crowd. "Taking Sakarig's youngest from him will not take the knife from your gut, Helmreik. It will not raise your son from the dead."

Helmreik gripped me harder, but his anger did not affect his voice. "Roman or Goth, no man's position frees him from his duty to the gods. This is about justice. Blood for blood," he said. "The boy spilled it. The boy owes it in return."

"That is not for you to say," Dagmar said, but it was lost in a rush of noise.

"Quiet," Helmreik bellowed to the clans, and they hushed enough to hear their reiks. "Our noble prince is right."

The Tervingi boys scoffed.

Dagmar looked confused, Adalgar suspicious.

My mother closed her eyes. She was praying.

The Tervingi boys jeered, and Helmreik smiled at them patiently. "We are but men," he said to them. "We are not in a position to know the will of Tiews." He made a show of bowing to the Angel on her blanket. To Dagmar, he said, "Or are you wiser than the runes?"

What could Dagmar say to this? Nothing. Nor the elder-men. Nor Adalgar. The prince looked trapped. He opened his mouth, closed it, and shook his head.

Helmreik said, "Then we are agreed."

Out of the corner of my eye, I saw Tanfrid nudge Fredo.

Helmreik raised his free arm to the sky. "I call upon the Angel of Death to read the runes. Let Tiews alone tell us what is to be done."

Vigdis the Apprentice placed a hand on the Angel's shoulder, and the priestess opened her watery eyes. The girl leaned down to the old woman's ear.

Helmreik and Tanfrid were about to get what they wanted.

"Wait!" I spun away from Helmreik and sprinted to the priestess before anyone could stop me.

I was probably breaking countless sacred rules, but I didn't think about that.

"Don't listen to her," I beseeched the hunched woman. "*You* read the runes. Just you. That's the law. *You're* the Angel of Death. Not *her*." I pointed to Vigdis. "Whatever you read, I will do. I swear it."

It took a long time—days and days, by my reckoning—for the Angel to respond, to show she had heard.

Vigdis bristled, her lips moving soundlessly as she rolled small willow branches between her fingers.

The crowd jostled.

Tanfrid would have come after me, but Helmriek pushed him back.

My mother tried to force her way past the eldermen. Adalgar blocked her.

It wasn't courage that kept me from running to her, but fear. I looked from my mother to Adalgar to my brother, my feet frozen in place. Karig's attention wasn't on the Angel or me. He was staring at Tanfrid with murder in his eyes.

Finally, the Angel pulled a hand-sized bag from beneath her robes. She mumbled her words and tipped the bag so bits of wood, slashed with the symbols of the gods, scattered over the blanket.

Vigdis lifted the hem of her tunic to kneel down. "Don't listen," she whispered. "The boy is guided by evil spirits."

She tried to take the priestess by the arm, but the old woman grunted and slapped the girl's hand away. The Angel bent over the runes, so far over I thought she would topple and mash her face into the ground. Her fingers groped the carved figures on each of the shaved twigs, first one, then another. She pulled a single piece from the pile and held it up the same way she had held the doomed bird.

"The rune of Tiews," she rasped. "The high god demands that the stone carrier receive the mark of justice. The stone carrier owes a raven's worth of blood. This debt will be paid. Prepare the sacrifice."

SACRIFICE

ONLY A RAVEN'S worth of blood. That didn't seem so bad. Not death. My courage returned.

Helmreik took hold of me again, perhaps expecting me to run from the Angel's knife.

My mother crossed over to us and flashed her hazel eyes at the Tervingi reiks. "Let him go."

Helmreik's grip faltered with her approach, then tightened again. "You've stepped too high, Fenja."

Tanfrid came up beside us, crossed his arms and smiled down at her.

She ignored Tanfrid and spoke to Helmreik. "His own people will hold him. He deserves that much."

"That is not for you to say."

My mother closed the distance between them and lowered her voice to a quiet, smooth, deadly tone, a tone that prickled the hairs on the back of my neck. She placed a hand on my free shoulder. I sucked in a breath involuntarily.

"You have done what you set out to do," she said to

Helmreik. "There is no stopping this now. Not without war, and you have the numbers on your side. We are not in a position to argue." She cast a look in Dagmar's direction. "But you will give me my son, or—numbers or no—there will be extra sausage and dumplings at tomorrow's break-of-fast." She cocked one eyebrow, then added, "I will use your irreverent son's knife."

I didn't get her meaning, but Helmreik seemed to understand. He flushed red.

Without waiting for his answer, she pulled me toward her, away from Helmreik.

"Take the vermin." He shoved me the rest of the way. "You think you've outrun death?" he said to me. "Death has stood on your shoulder from the day you were born, boy." He ran frosty eyes over my mother. "He doesn't need to die for the people to see that Greuthungi fortunes have changed. He will bleed in front of them. That will be enough. The gods are no longer on Sakarig's side." Helmreik waved a hand dismissively and turned his back on us.

"How did you know he had a knife?" was all I could think to say.

I watched the fat Balthi spit orders at Tanfrid, nostrils flared, neck veins popping. He'd spoken in a smooth, controlled way to us, but the Tervingi reiks was angry.

Good.

I was proud of my mother. No one got the best of her in a fight, and she didn't even have to hit anything.

Around us, clansmen had begun to push and shout, order breaking down. I looked to my mother, to smile, to show her I was able to take this punishment. A cut or two.

Karig had done worse to me, I told myself, until I saw the panic on her face.

"Prepare the sacrifice," a Terving said.

"Wash him down…"

"…Enough words…"

"…Before the noon sun."

My mother pulled me away from the worst of the commotion as boys hauled a thick tree stump to the center of the meadow and placed it in front of the Angel. There were rules to the sacrifice, and the morning was slipping away.

One boy shoved another somewhere in the mass of bodies. A fight broke out; the crowd repositioned.

A stone clipped my leg. A Terving woman captured her young son by his tunic with one hand and gave him a slap with the other. The boy had used the stone as a weapon within the sacred place, a slight against the gods unless under attack. The boy rubbed his face where her hand had struck him. He was smaller than me, no more than six years, but glared at me with the hate of an enemy.

My mother knelt down and opened her mouth to say something. No words came out.

"Don't worry," I said to her. "I'll hold still."

I saw tears escape the corners of her eyes and was confused.

"It's all right, mother," I said. "Only a raven's worth of blood." I was bare-chested and cold. My body shook.

"Yes," she whispered and wrapped her arms around me. "You'll be fine."

"He won't survive it," Old Woman Alba, our clan witch, mused. "No man has ever survived the cut of the Angel's knife. Cursed, it is. She spits on the blade with her venom."

"Alba," Aunt Brunehild snapped as she waddled over to us. She placed a hand on my mother's hair.

Alba clucked. "Suit yourself. I'll boil up the mugwort, but I'm telling you, you'll just be prolonging the inevitable. Bring him to the healing place as soon as the Angel's done with him." She elbowed through the crowd in the direction of our longhouses.

My insides began to twist.

Karig came to stand beside our mother. "Helmreik wouldn't dare if father were here. If the fighting men were here, they'd fry up his hind-cheeks for a feast."

"Hush," our mother said. "Get Adalgar. Tell him to select someone to help him hold Matthi."

"I can hold him," Karig said. "I'll get Keld to take the other side." And he disappeared through the waiting bodies before our mother could argue.

"Remember," she said to me. "You promised to hold still. Don't make the cut worse by moving. When it's over, don't fight or make a show. We must return to the longhouse, to Alba —"

She was still speaking when a giant hand landed on my shoulder. "It's time," Adalgar said.

My mother nodded and released me. I heard her calling for Karig as Adalgar guided me through a sea of bodies.

A hand smacked my ear. A foot struck my leg. An elbow caught me in the chin and my teeth cut into my cheek. I tasted blood.

"Let us pass," Adalgar grumbled, protecting me even as he led me toward the Angel's knife. "The gods have said their piece. He's no good to Tiews if he's mashed up."

I looked up to Adalgar's hairy, scarred face.

"You got yourself in a pretty pickle," Adalgar said grimly.

"Is it true? Nobody's ever survived her blade?" Tears threatened to flow. I swallowed, blinked them back.

"That's what they say. Who knows if it's true."

We were almost to the Angel's blanket. Adalgar stopped and met my eye, an old soldier sizing me up. "You have the look of your mother."

I shrugged. "Everyone says that."

"But you use your head like your father. Fight like him, too."

I'd never been compared to my father before. A stupid tear slipped down my cheek. I swiped it away angrily.

Adalgar started me walking again. "Save me a seat at the Warrior's Table, if it comes to that."

My uncle released me so, when we reached the shrunken circle that held the Angel, I was standing on my own—trembling, terrified—but holding myself straight.

FIGURES AND FACES BLURRED around me.

Karig appeared with Keld and they took their positions at the tree stump next to the Angel of Death.

"Back away," Adalgar called out, and the circle widened. He motioned to me to come forward. I was to place my arm across the sawed top of the stump, Karig holding my wrist, Keld at my back in case I pulled away.

I swallowed back the vomit that rose from my gut, knelt beside the stump and offered up my arm. Adalgar nodded his approval.

"Hold it tight. Don't let them see me flinch," I whispered to Karig.

"You have my word." Karig placed his rune necklace in my hand and took hold of my wrist.

The crowd silenced. Birds chirped, filling the uneasy quiet.

The Angel of Death rose from her blanket and crossed to the stump. When she was near enough for me to smell her, Vigdis handed the priestess the sacrificial knife. The blade had not been washed. Bits of raven guts clung to the metal. The Angel slid the dull edge of the blade along the underside of my arm, showing the gods and the clansmen where she would make the cut. Crusted blood from the dead bird left a red trail as the Angel made her shaky way along my skin. The cut would be long. She traced a line from the inside of my elbow all the way down my forearm. At my wrist, she turned the knife first left, then right, to form the head of an arrow. I was to be marked with the sign of Tiews.

Karig held me tight. I could sense my mother nearby, but I didn't dare look at her, or I would lose my nerve. Instead, I crushed the rune in my fist, so the arrow point bit into my palm.

The Angel began her prayers.

Long prayers.

My whole body went cold. If Tiews was going to take me, he needed to get on with it. Make it quick.

The Angel held up the knife, as she had held up the bird. *Here it comes.*

When the knife came down, it came quick. It sank into my skin. Deep. And the Angel's words came with it. Those stupid, muttered words. At first, the pain wasn't so bad.

That surprised me. Almost nothing at all. But then it hit, sharp and overwhelming. I heard a scream, my scream, loud, long, until my breath was nearly gone and my chest felt tight.

No! You're shaming yourself. Shut your mouth.

My teeth clamped down hard onto my tongue, and blood choked me when I tried to inhale and spurted from my mouth onto Karig's face when I blew the breath out.

Karig was on his feet now, holding my arm down by the wrist with the full weight of his body. Keld had control of my shoulders; his knee pressed into my back. The Angel continued the cut. Down. Down. And I couldn't tear my eyes from the knife digging into my skin. I watched it, holding my tongue in my teeth until the black crept in around me.

THE WOLF

THE CLANSMEN WERE GONE. Karig and the Angel and my mother, too. I was alone with the wolf in the center of the empty meadow on the damp autumn morning.

The wolf had me. Fangs ripped into my arm. Spit dripped from black gums. The large, shaggy head twisted back and forth, tearing my flesh. It shifted its body backward and, step by step, drug me toward the tree line, where a shadow figure—a woman—waited for me with ghostly calm.

She beckoned, thin and pale. Moss—her only clothing—clung to her bony frame in patches. Matted black hair hung straight down, past her waist, her cheeks hollow, her eyes roach-black pits. Behind her, an endless vacant gloom that was no longer the forest I knew.

I resisted the pull of the wolf, but the more I fought against the locked jaw, the more pain flooded me.

Better to give in. I'd asked for a quick death. Why did I resist now?

Karig called from a distance. "Look at me, Matthi. I've got you."

For a moment, I balanced between the terrible light—mumbled words, the reek of rotting cabbage, my brother's protective eyes, screaming agony—and the somber peace of the dark.

The wolf snarled, yanked. I gave ground. The trees whispered. The figure reached out. She would embrace me, I was sure. She didn't speak, but her silence promised the end of pain.

"Matthi," I heard my brother again. "Open your eyes." It was a frantic order.

Karig was always bossing me around, ready to choke me out one moment and take a punch for me the next. He would not hesitate to trade places with me now, but this was not his fight.

I anchored my foot against a stone. The wolf clamped down harder, its full weight in its hind legs, and I pulled back and refused to budge.

"You'll have to come and get me!" I yelled to the shadow figure. "A raven's worth of blood. Only that. If you want more, you'll have to come out and fight."

She stood motionless.

"Well then," I said, and wasn't afraid of her anymore.

I wrenched my arm from the mouth of the beast. The wolf snapped once, growled, then sniffed the air, whined and drew back.

When I turned to the open meadow, a second figure took shape in the mist where the Angel and Karig and the stump had been. Half shadow, half man, he was cloaked in aged deer hide, a grey beard grown full to his chest, eyes like ice, face webbed with battle scars and only a stub where his left hand should have been.

I blinked, tried to bow my head, but couldn't. The high god—the god of battle and courage and justice—filled the open space. His stub of an arm hung at his side, and I could not tear my eyes away from it.

I knew the story better than any other. The story of the great wolf—son of the Trickster, brother to Hel—who grew so big and hungry and untamable, he threatened to devour the world.

The gods had a special rope fashioned, forged from the sound of a cat's footsteps, the roots of mountains, the spittle of birds—things that do not exist and so cannot be fought— and challenged the wolf to a test of strength. The wolf, suspecting a trick, would only agree to the test if one among the gods would lay a hand in the beast's mouth as a pledge of good faith. Knowing this would mean the loss of the hand and a breaking of an oath, none of the gods agreed. Finally, Tiews, for the good of all, placed his hand in the giant jaws.

"You held your hand in the wolf's mouth," I said to the figure. "Held it still, while they bound him."

And when the gods refused to release the beast, the wolf realized he had been tricked and snapped his jaw closed. Tiews had sacrificed the hand—and the great wolf lost his freedom—and the world survived.

I looked down at my forearm, bloody and burning.

Was that what was being asked of me? To keep my arm in the mouth of the beast and lose it as Tiews had lost his? Was this the mark of which the Angel had spoken?

I would be called a one-handed cripple for the rest of my

life, seen as half a man in battle, and this scared me more than facing Hel.

From the meadow, Tiews watched me, judged me, as he judges all moments of courage and cowardice. The high god didn't speak; he didn't have to. My mistake and my promise to the Angel were debts. I could stand behind my actions now, or the great beast would collect payment from my clan later.

Tiews waited.

I hoped my fear wouldn't count against me. "If I owe it," I said, "I will give it."

The great, one-armed shadow returned to the mist.

The wolf whined again.

I faced the beast, held out my arm and prepared for the jaws to grab hold.

It didn't come closer. Instead, it drew away, raised its head and howled into the gray air.

Near the tree line, Hel was gone, too.

Stupefied, I turned to the light and was back at the stump, blade halfway down my forearm, blood trickling from the cut onto the wood.

Karig was there, flushed, wide-eyed, frantic.

Scared.

Karig was scared.

Around us, there was a fluster of scattered sounds and movements.

The crowd was unsettled again.

"I told Tiews he could have it," I tried to say to Karig because I thought the worshippers had lost faith in me.

My tongue felt thick, and my voice didn't work. My

stomach heaved, and my head hung heavy. And the pain. The pain made it hard to see anything else but red.

In the distance, the wolf howled again. Only it wasn't the wolf. It was a horn. The watchman's horn. Two blasts. A pause. Then again.

"Romans," Keld said, indignant.

Roman soldiers rarely appeared on our lands, and never neared our longhouses. My father said the Goths were allowed to govern themselves, and Romans were not a threat to us.

But everyone knew a religion called Christianity was the law, and our gods were not welcome within Roman borders, so our ceremony, especially the knife in my arm, was illegal. Perhaps the legion had been sent to punish our pagan worship, maybe they would do harm to the Angel, but I couldn't think on this as the Angel tugged the blade down my flesh.

Our Eldermen were weaponless, except for walking sticks and Tanfrid's knife. Around me, clansmen reached for pebbles and sticks in the grass, which they were allowed to use against attack, but would be useless against Roman swords. The circle of worshippers broke as the Eldermen called the older boys to the tree line to head off the soldiers. Greuthungi and Tervingi had been about to tear each other apart. Now they moved together to face the intruders.

Helmreik ordered Tanfrid and Fredo to stand guard around the Angel and Vigdis. Several Eldermen, women and girls joined them.

I expected the Angel to stop cutting, but she hunched lower, mumbled faster, dug the knife in deeper as if the sacrifice were all that mattered in the world.

"Halt," came a command in the Goth language from somewhere beyond.

"We're surrounded," Keld repeated what he heard from the crowd. I felt him stretch to see. "Hundreds. Some on horseback."

"Dagmar, Ishild, Ermalinde!" Adalgar shouted to Keld to go with him to protect the prince and his sisters. I felt the knee at my back release. Keld was gone.

Karig still gripped my wrist, but I could pull away from the Angel if I allowed myself to move and this terrified me. I clutched the rune in my hand, but couldn't feel my fingers, couldn't make a solid fist.

"Don't leave me," I tried to say to Karig through the pain with my half-chewed tongue.

"I won't."

Karig held fast while elders and boys and women and girls from all the clans yelled and swore and fought the wave of red tunics who broke through the worshippers and shoved their way to the tree stump and the Angel.

Once there, soldiers formed a circle of their own, a human wall—shoulder to shoulder around the Angel, Vigdis, Karig and me—and pushed the clansmen outward. My mother called to us. She struggled with a soldier blocking her way.

The Angel continued to cut and mumble until a Roman reached for her feeble arm and pulled her back from her work at the moment she'd reached my wrist and had twisted the knife to one side to begin to make the arrow's head. The soldier stripped the blade from her hand, chucked it in the grass and drug the Angel away from the stump.

"No!" Vigdis shrieked. She lunged forward, swept up the

knife and—before Karig could stop her—sunk the tip deep into my bloody arm. She yanked it free and raised the knife to strike again. This time, Karig blocked her, shoved her away.

I screamed until I vomited. My body shook violently.

"You were to die," Vigdis raged and lunged again. "I saw it."

Arms closed around her. A soldier pulled her back, leaving Karig to grab me before I toppled over.

"Sit up," Karig said. His tunic was slashed through at the shoulder, a red stain formed.

"You touched her." I lisped. My tongue was swollen. I felt cold. The Angel of Death and her apprentice were never to be touched on penalty of death.

"She had no right." Karig fumbled with a piece of linen to tie my arm.

"They'll read against you."

"She's not the Angel."

I opened my hand, exposing Karig's rune, a movement that sent bolts of pain through me. When I caught my breath, I said, "take it."

Karig shook his head. "After."

"Take it," I said again. My teeth chattered. Karig slid the rune from my palm and tucked it in his belt.

Beyond the Roman circle, women spat curses. Old and young Goths from both sides of the field rushed weaponless at the intruders. Tanfrid and Fredo broke through the red wall and charged toward the Angel to protect her.

The Angel's captor was a young soldier, clean shaven, skin flushed and soft looking, like a maiden. The fresh-faced legionnaire was smaller than Tanfrid, and one arm was busy with the Angel, who thrashed and scratched. He should have been no match for the two Balthi, but the soldier used his shield to block, before ramming the iron-clad edge against Tanfrid's already swollen chin. In the same motion, the soldier swept the shield back and landed the opposite edge into Fredo's elbow. Both Tanfrid and Fredo vanished from the circle before I knew what happened to them.

The Angel continued to screech and froth. She tried to get back to me, but the young soldier lifted the frail old woman off the ground, her feet flailing uselessly in the air. A second Roman had hold of Vigdis, her arms crossed in front of her and locked in place. Vigdis stopped fighting and focused her curse-filled eyes on me.

"The mark!" the Angel screamed. "I must finish!" She wheezed and coughed and tried to scratch the hand holding her.

The young legionnaire did not pay her any attention. He held the Angel like she were a piece of trash.

Karig finished wrapping the strip of linen around the top of my arm, then yanked, tightening the knot.

"Ow."

"Shut up."

A soldier stepped aside and allowed my mother through the circle. She pushed past the soldier, ran to us and knelt in the grass beside me. She'd torn material from her fine tunic and pressed it hard against my cut.

"Ah!"

"Don't move." She worked without emotion, except for the tears drying on her cheeks.

"What's happening?" I slurred. My tongue hurt almost as much as my arm. I was tired, head light, stomach churning, but I'd never seen Roman soldiers close up. Now they were everywhere. Fascinated, a bit afraid, a bit relieved, I fought the urge to sleep.

"They are here to stop the sacrifice," Karig said bitterly. "We must have no gods but their gods."

"Be silent and do what they say," our mother murmured.

"Is this my fault?" I swallowed blood. "I told Tiews he could have it. The Angel said…"

"Hush," she said, and pressed harder on my wound. "You have given enough."

A DEAL STRUCK

I COULD HEAR hooves pounding in the meadow and the clink of metal coins on horse tack.

Karig gathered a handful of stones, stood and prepared to throw.

"Drop them," our mother whispered as she spun linen around my mangled wound.

My attention was evenly divided between the blinding burn of the cut, the squeeze of the bandage and the Roman's in the meadow.

"Roman scum." Karig unleashed the stones before throwing himself at the nearest soldier. He'd landed a solid blow, but within two breaths, he was face down in the grass, mouth tasting dirt, three legionnaires pinning him to the earth.

My mother continued to press the cloth against my wound, prayers falling faster from her lips.

"Karig," I wanted to help him.

"No." She yanked me back, and my cut sang. She leaned

closer to me and whispered, "Be calm and do what you're told. They won't hurt him."

She sounded sure.

I wasn't so sure.

I watched Karig twist under the knees and hands that held him. "How do you know?"

"Quiet." It was a firm and desperate order. Reluctantly, I held still as she tied my bandage tight and knotted it. I tried to keep silent, to endure. It was no use. A moan shot from my belly out of my mouth.

Beside us, the Angel raged. I heard her, but couldn't see her anymore. I only saw my mother and red tunics and red blood, until the soldiers parted and a Roman headman on a fine gray mare looked down on us.

I recognized the mare. She was Greuthung, bred in our Amal stables, sold to the Roman Legion for a year of grain and supplies. Now she stood against the clan who raised her, head high like royalty, hide shimmering in thin patches of morning sunlight, her tack adorned with copper coins.

"*Wolke*," I mouthed. Karig had named her.

Wolke drew closer. Close enough to lower her head between my mother and me. I touched the hair of her mane. Her copper coins jangled, and I held one between my fingers.

The headman loomed over us.

Karig cursed and shouted from the dirt.

Beyond the circle, bodies clashed, rocks pelted against shields. Inside the circle, time stopped. The Roman headman dismounted.

"Fenja, wife of Sakarig?" the headman asked in our Goth language. My mother nodded without moving her eyes from me. Blood had already soaked through the cloth. "You and your sons will come with me."

Her brow creased; her lips pursed. "Gaius?" she whispered.

"Yes."

Gaius. It was the name I had heard earlier that morning in the longhouse, and I looked from the headman to my mother.

"You will take my son to the Greek," she said, then turned her face up to the headman.

"Yes," the headman called Gaius said. "We must hurry."

To a second horseman, he said, "Take him, Simeon. When we clear the trees, ride on ahead."

My mother drew me to her and whispered, "Don't fight."

She released me to the red tunics who lifted me up to a gruff, compact legionnaire—Simeon—who sat me in front of him as I kicked and yelled.

Gaius shouted orders in Latin, a language I'd heard my father speak, but didn't understand. The young soldier who held the Angel deposited her in the arms of two Tervingi women. Vigdis was released and left on her own to hug herself and seethe.

From my new seat, I could see the whole meadow. Legion guards stood at intervals around the edge of the clearing, blocking escape, shields raised. A few clansmen lay wounded in the grass; a few fought wildly.

If this were a real attack men would be dead. The soldiers weren't after blood. But on the back of Simeon's horse, his arm like an iron cuff around me, this didn't matter to me.

The Romans had separated Prince Dagmar and his sisters and Helmreik and his sons from the crowd. The royals were as trapped by the invaders as I was. Soldiers corralled the rest of the clansmen to one side of the meadow, creating a direct route to the forest path whenever Gaius was ready to take it.

"That'll teach 'em to leave their weapons in the barn," Simeon said in accented Goth.

On the ground beneath *Wolke* and Gaius, the three soldiers pinning Karig allowed him to rise. Karig sprayed the smallest soldier with a handful of rocks and followed it up with a head-butt, which caused no damage because Karig was a hand-width shorter. The other two legionnaires tried to subdue him again. Karig kicked one in the groin, wrestled the soldier's shield away from him and smashed it against the third. Soon, Karig was swimming in red tunics again.

"No!" I yelled.

I squirmed against my captor in the saddle.

"Easy now," Simeon said. "He'll be all right."

I kicked again. I cursed. I arched my back, and my head slammed against the breastplate behind me. Simeon gripped my bandaged arm, and I screamed out and kicked harder and heard my mother snapping at me to calm down.

Simeon squeezed. Hard. He pressed his calloused thumb down on my wound. "Sit still," he said calmly.

The legionnaire was too strong. My head spun.

"Karig!"

The young soldier who had dared hold the Angel stepped into the fight. Within two moves, Karig was on the ground again. This time, someone supplied a rope, and they tied Karig's legs and hands. The legionnaires hoisted my brother, arse-up, over the back of a waiting horse.

I twisted, tried to get to Karig, to my mother.

Hopeless.

Simeon chuckled. "Like father, like son."

Gaius signaled. A horn sounded.

The horsemen galloped across the meadow, slowed their horses to a walk down the narrow path through Hel's forest, then picked up speed when they reached the open fields, across Greuthungi farmland, past the longhouses.

Simeon pulled away from the pack. Soon, he and I were on our own, sprinting along well-worn trails, over a rolling hill, then two or more miles down the great Roman Road that led to the walled city of Oescus.

Here, Simeon slowed, but only a little to save his horse.

In defiance of my light head and Simeon's grip, I had fought until we were well away from Goth lands. I'd never been outside the borders of my laeti, and panic kept me going.

"You keep fightin' me, you're gonna be feelin' the bite of it all the way to the garrison," Simeon said. It was a statement of fact, not a threat.

"Where are we going? Where's my mother? Where's Karig?" I was not ready to admit defeat, but the urge to sleep covered me like a fog. Worn down, I leaned back against the breastplate and let my limbs go slack.

Simeon released my arm. "Your mother and brother are fine. They're behind us. I'm taking you to Oescus, to the garrison. You'll be needin' the Greek."

"I don't want to go to a Greek." I didn't know what that was. "Why did you come? Was it because of the ceremony? Are you against our gods?"

Simeon laughed. "We came for you and your family. A deal's been struck. That's all I know. It's over my rank."

"What deal?"

"Something better than the one we plucked you from."

"My father will find you and gut you." It came out with less spite than I intended. "Weapons are forbidden at the sacrifice. We were unarmed."

"Seems like a pretty smart time for us to show up then," he said.

He spat out a tangle of red hair that had flown in his mouth when I turned my head. "You need a bath and a shearing, son. Can't tell if you're a boy or a girl?"

I elbowed the legionnaire with my good arm. My funny bone hit metal.

He chuckled again. "Guess you'll be rid of those locks soon enough. If the Greek doesn't scrub you down, the trainers will."

"Trainers?"

"Sons of high-ranking legionnaires go to the military academy within the garrison."

I squirmed again, a weak, futile gesture. "My father is not a legionnaire. Goths don't have to go until seventeen. That's the law." I drifted. It was hard to focus. My eyes closed. "I don't want to go to an academy."

"How do you know what you want? You only know one thing."

"You can't make me." I blinked to keep myself awake. "And what about our mother?"

"By the Governor's decree, as the wife of Sakarig, she'll be given rooms inside the city walls." Simeon sounded like he was quoting something he'd heard. "It's been ordered that you and your brother and mother be held under Roman control so long as your father leads the Goth auxiliary forces."

We rode a few moments in silence. Simeon touched my bandage which dripped blood on the man's leggings. "A nasty bit of work."

"I dropped the plate," I slurred. I tried to lift the arm and failed, "It's only a line, not an arrow. She wasn't finished. I owed it. A raven's worth of blood."

"She might not have finished the line, but on my word, you gave the blood. Twice that, I'd wager."

Simeon spurred the horse on.

Somewhere among the patches of trees and gentle swells in the land, the wolf followed us. Hel whispered on the wind. Her breath took hold of my bones. I trembled and fought the drowsy black and didn't remember the last bit of road, the last moments of my life outside the great stone walls that would separate my new life from my old.

THE GARRISON

355 AD

AGAIN

How long has it been since the last horn? Is this the fifth water break? Sixth?

No resting.

I can't afford to give the others hope, so I don't allow myself to lean against the fountain stones or bend to stretch my back. I take my turn at the water spout and join the inspection line, shoulders squared, and assess the condition of the other cadets.

Next to me, Cato's sword hand trembles; a moan wheezes out of him. Lastimus shoves Jason the Beardless from the fountain. Jason doesn't fight back even though he outweighs Lastimus by a stone. Is Jason tired? Not really. He lacks a backbone, but his feet and wind look fine. Thomas wretches in the dirt, and maybe it will be him that quits first, maybe the trainers will end it for him, but I don't have it in me to hope for that. No-Neck Nonius takes his time at the spout. When his square head surfaces, his olive skin has a sickly sheen. He'll vomit in a few rounds.

Good.

Ionius mutters something about my mother as he passes. I take heart. Desperation is in the air. Someone is going to drop soon.

Fatigue hangs heavy on my limbs. I inventory the worst of it and ignore the rest.

Lastimus finishes at the spigot and saunters to his place in line. I grant him a grudging respect. He has mettle. If Lastimus quits first, it'll be because he's unconscious.

Or he can't walk, Karig whispers.

Shut up.

Smash his toes, first chance you get. Use the shield's edge. See if he's smiling then.

To smash toes, gouge eyes, or bash the head or neck with full force is to go against the rules of training. I'll win nothing if I cheat.

He'd do it to you.

In my mind, I punch my brother in the mouth, but the punch has no power.

Is that the best you got? May as well be slapping him with a dead rabbit.

I'm not cheating.

He's laughing at you. He's never going to quit.

Maybe not. But I don't need Lastimus to quit. Only one cadet needs to fall. Someone will break soon. I can feel it.

I face my opponent again.

Lastimus is the third son of a Roman senator, the only cadet to come from outside the province of Lower Moesia.

The garrison at Oescus, and the swelling city that shares a wall with the garrison, rests two miles from the banks of the great Danubius River. A man can't go farther north and still be under Roman law. To cross the river is to step out of the Roman Empire into the dark, savage-filled northland wilderness, where pale-skinned natives sacrifice their enemies to bloodthirsty gods, and a man's soul has no chance for Christian salvation. That's how the garrison priest describes it.

Lastimus was sent to train at Oescus when he was ten—why? no one could say—sponsored by his uncle, a noble-man, the richest landholder in the region.

"A frontier hick," Lastimus calls his uncle and refers to Oescus—the largest city within a hundred miles—as "the armpit of the Roman Empire." The senator's son spent his first years in a seaside town along the Mediterranean. He's been to Rome, has seen a spectacle inside the Colosseum. Lastimus doesn't speak much of his old life—as far as I've heard—but when he does speak, the cadets hang on his every word.

But Lastimus isn't the usual weak-spleened nobleman's son. Too bad. He's mean. He has a steady, cruel optimism that seems to leech energy from pain.

To our left, Blasius slips. His sword hilt smashes into the side of his opponent's head. A short, compact boy named Lucius is carried to the Greek. Lev saw the strike and gives Blasius a demerit.

The ticket was not justly earned. The drills continue.

Stensius the Gepid, a brooding, dirty-blond half-breed with steel blue eyes, moves to stand across from Blasius.

In all my years inside the garrison, I've never heard Sten-sius the Gepid speak. Sten's father is dead. His Gepid mother is tall and voluptuous and beautiful. That makes Sten's life in the barracks hard. Cuts and bruises frequently mark his chiseled face and today is no exception. A cut under Sten's right eye had almost healed, but someone has reopened it, and I can't help studying it.

Sten's nostrils flare as if he can sense me staring, but the Gepid doesn't turn his head.

Keep your snot nose out of it, little brother, Karig sniffs.

"Looking good," Blasius says to his new partner.

When Sten doesn't respond, Blasius adds, "How's your mother?"

But Sten is immovable. He pretends not to hear Blasius and locks his eyes on Master Trainer Cassian, who crosses behind our drill line before meeting again with Lev. Maybe that is the only way to handle a thug like Blasius. Ignore him. But I know Sten is listening. There is rage in his eyes.

"She must be lonely, now that Manius has shipped out. He's gone to Durostorum, right?" Blasius checks to make sure the master trainer is out of earshot. "I've heard the watchmen are drawing lots to see who gets to share her bed next."

Around them, cadets shift, snort, smirk. This is a welcome distraction. Only Jason the Beardless and Thomas have the good manners to appear uncomfortable.

"It'll have to be someone, right? Better she has a protector than to sell her sagging body for crumbs on the street. Or will that be your sister's job."

For a moment, I imagine Sten breaking Blasius down right there in the arena in front of the trainers. It'd be worth the whipping. And Sten could do it, too. He's smart and, for all his chiseled beauty, he's a ruthless fighter. But Sten is cold-blooded, not hot-headed. He keeps his eyes forward.

A small part of me is disappointed.

"Same drill," Lev orders and calls out the opening strike. *"Caedare."*

Lastimus swings overhead and down, a hacking strike. He's not the largest cadet, but he's a good fighter without obvious weaknesses. And unlike Thomas, the wiry rat keeps light on the balls of his feet, shifting and dancing. His hawk-like eyes are focused, his strikes accurate and delivered with force. If Lastimus is tired, he isn't showing it.

Befuddled, I take two steps out of position and feel the sting of Lev's training stick against my outer thigh. By the time we finish the round, I can feel the welt under the thin fabric of my leggings. The muscles in my left upper thigh twitch. When I bend to steady the shake with my hand, my head swirls and a wave of nausea washes over me. My chest grows icy.

I straighten quickly, but it's too late. Lastimus can see my condition, and he's calculating how to punish me harder. The best I can do is duck and evade as I searched my opponent for some advantage.

Blasius sniggers at me, loses focus, and Sten smashes his spatha down hard on Blasius' shoulder. Blasius shakes it off, laughs, but his next blow misses. His timing is off.

Master Trainer Cassian paces on top of his wood platform overlooking our training lines, repeating the lesson again and again.

"Endurance," he rasps "Discipline." There is a cadence to his words. "A soldier can win a single fight with power, speed or aim. But, if you are good enough, and lucky enough, to survive the first few moments of battle, endurance and discipline will be your surest weapons. Like your sword or your spears, your shield and your shoes, they must be maintained, or they will fail you when you need them most."

He preaches discipline and endurance often. Preaches it so it has been carved on our hearts. Today, he makes us taste it, like the sweat that rolls into our mouths.

"Stop."

The last round has gone on past the point of counting, and my lungs clutch at me. My legs tingle, both twitching now. A spasm takes hold. I'm suddenly drained and have to remind myself to stand tall. My chest sinks on its own.

I try to master my breathing as Lev passes. For a moment, I'm so dizzy I feel myself tilt to the left. I'm floating. My fingers grip the rough handle bolted to the inside of my shield to anchor to something solid.

"Spatha up. Shield close. Step left. Again."

Lastimus hardly looks tired. Looks like he could go on for hours. Doubt pricks the back of my mind. I try to shut it out.

"Stop." Pause. "Again."

I reduce my world to simple thoughts. The next step, only that. I raise my shield high, keep the spatha low. Move my feet. Pick them up so I can't feel them slide through the dirt. Another callous strips off my hands. My right palm is slick with blood.

A raven's worth of blood?

The white line running down my forearm is so much a part of me, I don't notice it anymore. What makes me think of it now? The Angel of Death ambles over to my ear. She hisses her ancient words, and I swear her spittle lands on my cheek, the way it did when I was eight years old in the meadow. Behind me, the wolf waits to pounce.

"Stop."

I blink sweat from my eye.

"Again," Lev calls.

One more round, I chant to myself, but the fight is leaving me. One more step forward. One more swing.

And I lock against Lastimus, expecting to fall. The only thing keeping me up is the mass of my opponent.

You gonna quit, little brother?

Maybe.

"How's your endurance, pebble head?" Lastimus whispers.

Behind the taunt, a tremor. A whiff of desperation.

Lastimus should have kept his mouth shut.

I raise my shield so he won't see the sides of my mouth turn up. The senior presses his weight against the shield face forcing me back. "How's that discipline?" he says.

"Stop," Lev orders. "Backs straight."

Lastimus shoves me away, returns to the drill line and smiles like he's struck a wicked blow.

I shuffle into position, make a show of it, of squaring my shoulders, then of slumping again. Lev's training stick licks my back, and I falter but breathe in the sting and take another look at my opponent; the spasm in his left thigh; the jagged rise and fall of his chest.

Lastimus is wearing down.

"Again."

"You're good at keeping your head, eh," Lastimus starts in again on the first strike. "Better than your brother."

It's my turn to shove, because that's what a brother should do. Lastimus laughs at the feeble return.

"You look the part, you know. Of a cadet. Almost like you

belong here. Except for that red mop, of course. You talk Roman, walk in a straight line. You fight by the rules, don't you?" Then, when we part and come together again, "Your brother was savage to the bone. Not like you. No such thing as a fair fight to Karig, was there?"

"Stop."

No, there wasn't. But I'm not taking in the words. I'm watching feet, and how he drags his now, and isn't bouncing anymore.

"Again."

"You know, I almost won against him once." Lastimus is short of breath. The heckling is keeping him on his feet. Those slowing feet. The sloppy turns. With each move, he continues to goad me. Except the goading turns into something serious.

"Sparring. I was two years younger than him. New senior, just like you. Well, you're not a senior yet, right?" Lastimus blinks. Shakes his head, like he's shaking off a haze. I move him left, then right. He lunges at me, talking. "And Karig was tough. And mean. But Karig wasn't good for keeping his head. And I was staying out of his way, mostly. Shifting. Moving. And your brother, well, he was getting worked up. I would have won, you know..."

I can sense what's coming, because it's what Karig would have done if he lost his temper, if he were about to be beaten. And Lastimus has carried the anger around for years, hasn't he? Karig didn't know how to lose a fight. Didn't believe in rules. Would have rather faced the lash than face defeat. I can see what Lastimus plans in the upturn of that terrible, crooked smirk.

He comes at me, shield raised to block the trainers' line of sight. He drops his sword to the dirt to free his hand and reaches around to grab hold of the back of my neck, to pull me forward, to crush my face with the bone of his forehead.

But Lastimus isn't Karig.

His timing isn't as good as Karig's was, and neither are his instincts. I lower my chin to my chest. Instead of a head-butt, Lastimus cracks his nose against hard skull, the top of my head.

"Ah!" Lastimus stumbles two steps backward, seizes his spatha from the arena floor and comes at me, the strike raining down from above. I raise my shield, my arms finished. When his spatha hits my shield, both shield and sword drop down on my head, driving me to the ground.

The hard earth meets me. I lose my wind. My throat constricts. No air. When I try to rise, my arms betray me. They won't hold my weight.

Is this it?

Vaguely, I hear Lev call a stop. If I can't rise on my own steam before a trainer reaches me, the day will be over. I'll earn a ticket to the Greek. The wiry rat, Blasius and the other seniors, will get what they want.

My pride, and my brother, scream at me to move my backside up off the dirt. At the same time, I feel my father rest a strong, warm, steadying hand on my chest.

What's your hurry? my father whispers.

You're right. Why get up at all? —I can't look at him, even in my mind.—*I'm finished.*

Are you?

Nearly.

That's not the same thing as finished.

What's the point? As fast as I get up, he'll drop me back down.

That will be then. This is now. Eat from the plate in front of you, son.

I let my head fall back, and my limbs go slack. My throat unlocks, and my breath returns. I'm breathing again, but I feel like death.

What a day.

I roll to my side and push myself up from the arena floor with my uncertain arms.

I manage to gain a knee when a hand reaches down.

I look up, addled.

The outline of Thomas leans over me, blocking what's left of the afternoon light.

"Get off your lazy arse, slacker," he says, sucking in air between each word. He's shaking, twitching, but he's still standing, and that's more than me.

I smile. "You're out of formation." I grab his hand. The effort nearly brings us both down.

Nearly.

One more round, I tell myself.

The master trainer doesn't call another round.

Blood flows freely from Lastimus' nose down his chin.

"I'm good," Lastimus says to Lev, and maybe we'll continue on, except, down the line, Cato collapses to the dirt, grips his leg and wails. No-Neck Nonius heaves. He pukes while standing at attention. Bile seeps from the sides of his mouth.

From his platform, Master Trainer Cassian gives his orders. "Cadets Cato, Nonius, Lastimus and Thomas, report to the infirmary."

"Yes, sir," the four say in unison.

"Thomas, upon your release, you will report to Senior Barracks B."

"Yes, sir." Thomas says with as much force as he can. He's made it. I try to maintain a stoic face, but fail.

"You four, dismissed."

Nonius lifts Cato, and the four exit out the west gate.

"Jason," the master trainer continues.

"Yes, sir."

"You will escort Matthias back to Junior Barracks C."

I blink. Absorb the words. *Junior Barracks C.* The master trainer has ordered me back to my old barracks. I can't help it. My head lowers. With enormous effort, I lift it again.

"Yes, sir," I hear Jason respond.

Master Trainer Cassian descends from the platform, stern, unreadable. He approaches, looks down at me, then over to Lev.

Maybe he'll tell me why I failed. Maybe he'll say I didn't get up in time or that I'm too small or that I'm not ready. Whatever the reason, I don't want to hear it, not in the arena with the others listening. It's stupid, but I want to cry. I won't let tears fall—not here, not ever—but feel them like little arrows at the back of my eyes. I wait for dismissal, and the humiliating walk to come.

The pause stretches on.

The master trainer folds his arms. His stance is more solid than the statue of Jupiter in the forum.

"Senior Cadet Matthias," he rasps. He addresses me in the same tone he's always used. I almost miss the change in title.

Senior Cadet Matthias. I'm too unsteady to be sure. It takes a moment for me to get words to come out. "Yes, sir."

"Retrieve your gear and that of Senior Cadet Thomas. Ready two bunks in Senior Barracks B, then report to the thermae."

Hot iron shoots through my limbs. "Yes, sir." I'm two feet above the ground, the tallest cadet in the drill line, all the energy in the world.

The master trainer dismisses us.

"Remaining Seniors," I hear as I follow Jason the Beardless out of the arena. "Bath, chow, rack. Training commences at dawn. Dismissed."

KARIG'S RUNE

My father isn't here to give his approval. Karig is silent, too. No ceremony. No pat on the back.

If I'd quit early on, the other seniors would be scrubbed, fed and playing dice by now. Instead, they'll be hungry, sore and bone-tired. They'll blame me for every ache and scratch.

Payback is coming. I don't care. I promoted. One small victory. Tomorrow, there will be a chance for another.

"Those two," Jason points to the bunks with bare mattresses against the far back wall and falls on his rack near the door to wait for me.

Senior Barracks B looks and smells exactly like my old junior quarters; two connected rooms and a terrace out back, creaky wooden floorboards and a moldy stench that no amount of lye can clean away.

To the left of the front door is the equipment room where I deposit Thomas' and my gear: two wooden spathas, two shields, six pila, and our summer garments. My arms are still shaking. It's a relief to unload.

To the right is the rack room, a long, narrow rectangle. It holds eight bunks—four up and four down—lined against one wall with a slim walkway leading from the entry down the bunk line. Three small windows let in enough light to see, but no more.

The sun has set, the day is dissolving fast. Across from the barracks, the torch lighters—three old slaves of mixed descent—ignite freestanding oil lamps on corners, and torches in holders hanging outside buildings along the most used streets. The torches will burn until after the evening meal.

A small lamp, flint and a steel rod rest on a low shelf near the connecting door of my new quarters, but I can see what I'm doing, so leave them untouched and make my way down the bunk line.

It's been years since I've racked so far from the door. There are walls on three sides. Not a lot of space. It's hard to breathe. If it weren't for the window across from the upper bunk, my head would be spinning. No way can I sleep with someone above me, too.

I make up the lower bunk for Thomas, then step on the bunk frame to take care of my bedding.

"You sure you want that one?" Jason asks.

It's a standard rack, exactly like all the others. "Karig's?"

"Uh, huh." Jason's half asleep.

I don't like the idea of sleeping on my brother's old mattress, but it doesn't feel right to have anyone else on it either.

I keep working. My tunic sleeve lifts revealing the tip of the ever-present white line running down the inside of my arm, and I'm reminded again of what I've paid and what I owe.

"Shame about your brother," Jason mumbles.

He's being nice. No reason not to take a kind word when offered. But Jason has a soft voice, a compassionate tone, and it makes me want to pummel him into the ground. I don't want compassion. I don't want old memories.

"Yeah," I say and hope that will be the end of it.

"The bunk's been empty since…" Jason doesn't finish.

What can he say?…*since your brother tried to escape the garrison and drowned in the river.*

Instead he says, "Karig was tough,"

I jam the blanket into the back corner.

"Never saw him lose a fight," he yaps on.

I try to block him out.

"He was a good fighter, a real…"

"…but not a good soldier," I cut him off.

"No," Jason rolls over on his rack. He rubs his eyes and stares up at the slats above him. "No, guess not."

"He quit," I say, mostly to myself.

If Jason heard me, he doesn't show it. His eyes are closed. I'm sorry I said anything at all.

I haven't allowed myself to talk about my brother in the two years since the master trainer delivered the news of his death.

The day's training has stirred up dead voices and muddy emotions.

I return to my task. There's a way a soldier tends to his rack. No wrinkles, neat, squared away, every morning before muster for a thousand mornings. No thought required. I work methodically until I swoop a hand underneath the last corner of the mattress and feel a thin strip of leather catch on my fingers.

I know what it is before I see it. Maybe that's why my stomach lurches, and I stall before I pull my hand from under the mattress.

Jason's waiting, so I draw the strip of leather up and out and with it, Karig's forged rune.

Master Trainer Cassian said Karig's death was his own doing. Karig was a deserter, and he received no honors, no burial or funeral pyre. My brother's body was disposed of like other deserters, in a common pit without a marking or ceremony. No way for Tiews or any god to find him. The master trainer told me this without pity—one soldier to another—then went on training me as before. For that, he'd earned my undying gratitude.

I hold the forged arrow between my fingers

You know I didn't leave it behind, little brother.

I don't know anything. I didn't know you.

But I can't help asking, "Did Karig have any friends here?"

Jason has fallen asleep. He sits up and pumps his shoulders to wake himself. "Friends?" he says dumbly.

I return Karig's rune to its hiding place, smooth one last wrinkle and jump down to the floor. "Never mind." It's only a necklace. I'm tired. I'm being stupid.

Jason leads the way out of the barracks toward the baths. I follow, the day and the rune behind me.

The water is cold and dirty. I don't care.

"Sten," Jason says as slaves slough skin from our backs and I'm rolling in and out of sleep.

"Huh?"

"Stensius," Jason says again. "Karig would talk to Sten sometimes. Not a lot. Karig kinda kept to himself, you know. Sten's not a big talker either. But sometimes they'd hang out at the evening meal."

"Thanks," I say. I'm drifting off again. Thoughts of Karig and runes, vengeful priestesses and scheming kings, wolves and Hel—and the angry seniors I'll face at the evening meal—dissolve into the hot and cold of the bathhouse. The worst is over, I tell myself.

And for these precious minutes of peace, I believe it.

A NOTE TO READERS

Recommended for readers 12 and up, this YA historical fiction series offers realistic grit, hard choices, action, adventure and suspense.

Parents, rest easy. While there's plenty of fighting and blood, there's no gratuitous gore, modern swearing or mature content.

The Stone Eagle is written in short episodes and designed to be read in order.

This series is a work of fiction, but I've painted the Goth clans, the Roman legions, the weapons, the garrison, and Oescus City and it's surroundings as accurately as possible (with a Glossary and Cast of Characters in the back to help keep things straight). Any mention of emperors or other key historical figures, wars, religions or major political disputes are based on historical fact unless noted. Descriptions of roads, rivers and other terrain features are also as accurate as I could make them given the information available.

The Greuthungi and Tervingi Goths existed. Sadly, information about their day-to-day lives, religion and customs is sparse. However, there are historical references to these tribes serving in Roman auxiliary units in exchange for land (*laeti*). Roman sources also mention the practice of Roman officials taking the sons of powerful Goth leaders as political hostages to assure peace. These Goth sons were reportedly treated well. And, while Matthi is a fictional character, a boy with his family ties could easily have been raised, educated and trained by the Romans. Many in Matthi's position were eventually accepted into the legion ranks as citizens, some promoting to positions of power.

Even though I've done extensive research and made every effort to be true to history, I'm not a historian. I welcome you, dear reader, to question, comment, make suggestions or call me out.

To contact me, or for more information about the world of The Stone Eagle, visit my website at www.thestoneeagle.com.

CAST OF CHARACTERS

THE GARRISON

Cadets :

MATTHI/MATTHIAS - Senior initiate; son of Sakarig and Fenja; brother to Karig; raised on a Goth laeti inside the Roman Empire until the age of eight, when he was taken as a political hostage by the Romans legion at Oescus. (14)

THOMAS - Senior initiate; Matthi's friend; son of Gaius, the Camp Prefect (15)

BLASIUS - Senior cadet; loud and aggressive; Barracks B (17)

LASTIMUS - Senior cadet; a wiry rat; nephew to the richest noble in the Oescus area; Barracks B (16)

STENSIUS - Senior cadet; a brooding half-blood; son of a fallen legionnaire and a beautiful Gepid; a friend of Karig's; Barracks B (16)

CATO - Senior cadet; a whiner; Barracks B (15)

JASON - Jason the Beardless; senior cadet; the oldest cadet in Barracks B so he's supposed to be in charge (17)

NONIUS - No-Neck Nonius; senior cadet; 2nd oldest in Barracks B (17)

IONIUS - Senior cadet; Barracks A (15)

LUCIUS - Senior cadet; Barracks A (16)

DECIMUS - Lead cadet; Junior Barracks B (14)

REGIUS - Junior cadet; thick-limbed, strong-bodied, weak-spleened; when he quits, the juniors are dismissed.

Trainers:

MASTER TRAINER CASSIAN - an ox of a man; a war hero; head trainer of the Oescus garrison cadets

ASSISTANT TRAINER LEVIUS (LEV) - a Greuthungi Goth who has earned his citizenship and a respected post; lean and sinewed

Assistant Trainer Fabius - recently assigned to the Oescus garrison; in charge of the junior cadets.

Assistant Trainer Drusus - the youngest of the academy trainers; in charge of the youngster cadets.

Legionnaires:

Gaius - Father of Thomas; Camp Prefect of the Legion of the V Macedonica at the time of Matthi's initiation; Was the Roman officer who interrupted the Goth ceremony to take Fenja, Karig and Matthi back to the city

Simeon - A Roman soldier, under the command of Gaius, who carried Matthi to the garrison.

Mentioned (but not shown):

Paulopus the Greek - The old slave doctor who runs the infirmary within the garrison, the only real doctor within 100 miles.

The Priest - In charge of the religious and practical education of the cadets and all religious matters inside the garrison.

THE GOTHS

The Angel of Death - High Priestess of the Goths; born a Greuthung; Tiews is thought to speak through her. Her word is law.

Vɪɢᴅɪs - The Angel's apprentice. She will be anointed *Angel of Death* when the old priestess passes on. Vigdis was born a Terving. (12)

Greuthungi Goths:

Sᴀᴋᴀʀɪɢ ᴛʜᴇ Sɪʟᴇɴᴛ - Or Sakarig the Elder; father to Karig and Matthi; husband to Fenja; head of the Goth auxiliary unit; seen as the only man who can unite the hostile Northland Goth clans (mentioned but not shown)

Fᴇɴᴊᴀ - Mother to Matthi and Karig; wife to Sakarig

Kᴀʀɪɢ - Sakarig the Younger; brother to Matthi (12 at the sacrifice)

Aᴅᴀʟɢᴀʀ ᴛʜᴇ Fᴏʀɢᴇʀ - Father to Keldamar; uncle to Karig and Matthi; brother to Sakarig the Silent

Kᴇʟᴅᴀᴍᴀʀ (Kᴇʟᴅ) - Son of Adalgar; one of eight siblings. Cousin to Matthi and Karig; Karig's best friend (12 at the time of the sacrifice)

Pʀɪɴᴄᴇ Dᴀɢᴍᴀʀ ᴛʜᴇ Yᴏᴜɴɢᴇʀ - Son to the dead leader of the Greuthungi clans—Reiks Dagmar the Amal; Prince Dagmar is 13 at the sacrifice. The Angel of Death foretold he would lead the Northland Goths when he came of age.

Eʀᴍᴀʟɪɴᴅᴇ (Eʀᴍɪ) - Youngest daughter of Reiks Dagmar the

Elder; sister to Prince Dagmar and Ishild (Ermi is 9 at the sacrifice)

ISHILD THE BEAUTY - Eldest daughter of Reiks Dagmar the Elder; sister to Prince Dagmar and Ermalinde (Ishild is 11 at the sacrifice)

ALBA - the Village Witch (medicine woman)

AUNT BRUNEHILD - Sakarig's sister; aunt to Karig and Matthi

Tervingi Goths:

HELMREIK - Head of the Balthi clan; Reiks of the Tervingi; Father to Tanfrid and Leogern. He's lost his eldest son, who served under Sakarig in the auxiliary unit.

TANFRID - 2nd son of Helmreik, but his older brother is dead, making him the eldest; Brother of Leogern

LEOGERN - 3rd son of Helmreik; brother of Tanfrid

FREDO - Cousin to Tanfrid and Leogern

GODS (and otherworld creatures):

TIEWS *(Tee-ooz)* - High god of the Goths; God of War and Justice and Right Action; sacrificed his hand to the great wolf to save all humanity.

Nerthus - A fertility goddess; Goddess of the Harvest and Mothers

Hel - Goddess of the Underworld; daughter of the Trickster; sister to the Wolf

The Wolf - The Hound of Hel; Hel's brother; centuries later, Norse mythology refers to the wolf as Garm or Fenrir.

GLOSSARY

AUXILIARY UNIT - A non-citizen military unit which fought alongside the Roman legions in exchange for pay and eventual citizenship. However, by 355 AD, the terminology was fuzzy. Sakarig's unit of Goths would probably not have been called *auxiliary*. More likely they would have been a combination of *comitatenses*—high grade interception forces—and *limitanei*—lower-grade border troops. I use *auxiliary* for simplicity and flow.

BARRACKS - Military housing where the cadets, officers and trainers slept and stored their personal belongings. Usually, Roman soldiers cooked and ate their meals in/outside their barracks, too.

CAMP **P**REFECT - The second highest ranking officer in a legionary garrison. He reported to the commander of the legion—the legate. The camp prefect was in charge of basic legion organization, equipment and training. He could also command the legion in the absence of the legate.

CENTURION - A professional officer in the Roman Army; commander of a group of around 80 men (a century). Senior centurions could also take senior staff rolls and/or command multiple centuries.

CLAN - A group of people connected by a common ancestor; an extended family unit. The Goths would have called this unit a *kuni* (e.g. Matthi would have belonged to the Amal kuni). But, this story has several unfamiliar words and I chose to use the more modern word for simplicity.

GARRISON - Troops stationed in a particular location; home base; can be a town, castle, fort, ship, etc.

GEPIDAE - An Ancient Germanic group often associated with the Goths; In Gothic, Gepid means "slow ones."

GOTH - An Ancient (East) Germanic group of people thought to be of Scandinavian descent. Historians often break the Goths into two main groups: Visigoths and Ostrogoths, which is how Romans sources often referred to them. These groups controlled large areas to the north and west of the Black Sea before other tribes (e.g. Alani, Huns) pushed the goths south to the Danube River. Many modern scholars use the names Greuthungi (associated with the Ostrogoths) and Tervingi (associated with the Visigoths) to reflect how the Goths would have referred to each other. Again, another gray area.

GRENZ - The fictional name for the creek that marks the boundary of the **laeti** lands. *Grenz Creek* cuts through the north tip of *Hel's Forest*. The clans use the northern patch of forest to hunt and gather berries and wood, but do not venture south of the boundary.

GREUTHUNG (*PLURAL GREUTHUNGI*) - Once semi-nomadic Goths that controlled large areas north of the Black Sea. Greuthungi might translate as "steppe dweller" or "people of the pebbly coast." They may be the same people as the Ostrogoths. (Thank you Wikipedia and Peter Heather.)

LAETI - Land given to "refugees" within the Roman Empire, often in exchange for a pledge of service to the Roman army. On completion of their years of service, refugee soldiers could be granted citizenship for themselves and their children. Sources indicate the Romans allowed the inhabitants on laeti land to largely govern themselves.

LEGION - The largest unit of the Roman army. The size of a legion evolved over time. At the time of Julius Caesar, a legion had around 5000 men. In the 4th Century, the Legion of the V Macedonica (Oescus), might have contained no more than 1000 men.

OESCUS - A river (today Iskar) running through modern day Bulgaria, that feeds into the Danube (Goth: Danau; Latin: Danubius). The garrison and city were named for the river. Oescus garrison stood near where Gigen, Bulgaria stands today.

PILUM (*PLURAL PILA*) - A spear/javelin. Around two meters (six and a half feet) long. It had a two foot iron shank at the tip.

REIKS - A goth prince. This prince usually came from a "royal" family, but a reiks was considered "a first among equals." He held a leadership position by election.

RUNE - Letters/symbols used in Ancient Germanic cultures. Early examples are not standardized. Spears and shields with runic marking have been dated from 200 AD in Elder Futhark, the oldest form of the runic alphabets.

SPATHA - A longer sword; the blade was around 30 inches. It replaced the gladius (the shorter sword often seen in gladiator movies) as the standard legionary weapon.

TERVING (*PLURAL TERVINGI*) - Tervingi might mean "forest people" (thank you Wikipedia). Another translations is "people of the earth." They settled into a farming lifestyle in the plains northwest of the Black Sea. They might have been the same people as the Visigoths. (Thank you Peter Heather.)

THERMAE - Roman baths; a place not only to bathe, but to socialize and conduct business.

VERBODE - The fictional name given by the Goth clans for the land beyond their *laeti* border. Specifically, the *Verbode* is the name for the part of Hel's Forest to the south of the *Grenz.*

ACKNOWLEDGMENTS

The Stone Eagle would have suffered a slow and bloody death without the ongoing support of my husband, daughter, parents and brother.

Thank you also:

Ella, for many cups of tea in your cozy kitchen; Kris, for the first (gentle) edit; the Family Baca for your kind offer to beta read; Michael for tech advice and general enthusiasm; the Raven's Keep for writerly insights and encouragement, especially Tomas, for your endless knowledge of all things Goth and Roman; Magic for late night chats and story wisdom; and Luke for introducing me to *Truby* and the future or storytelling.

SO, HOW WAS IT?

I'd love to hear what you thought.

Please consider leaving a review. Reviews aide other readers in making informed reading choices and help authors better understand their audience.

You can also comment, make a suggestion or contact me on my website www.thestoneeagle.com.

Thank you.